INNOVATIVE TECHNOLOGIES

SOLAR ENERGY

ABDO
Publishing Company

INNOVATIVE TECHNOLOGIES

SOLAR ENERGY

BY CHRISTINE ZUCHORA-WALSKE

CONTENT CONSULTANT

Michael McGehee

Associate Professor, Materials Science and Engineering

Stanford University

CREDITS

Published by ABDO Publishing Company, PO Box 398166, Minneapolis, MN 55439. Copyright © 2013 by Abdo Consulting Group, Inc. International copyrights reserved in all countries. No part of this book may be reproduced in any form without written permission from the publisher. The Essential Library™ is a trademark and logo of ABDO Publishing Company.

Printed in the United States of America,
North Mankato, Minnesota

092012
012013

 THIS BOOK CONTAINS AT LEAST 10% RECYCLED MATERIALS.

Editor: Melissa York
Series Designer: Craig Hinton

Photo Credits: Shutterstock Images, Cover, 13, 14, 26, 76, 78, 83, 101; NASA/AP Images, 6; Dorling Kindersley/Thinkstock, 9; Red Line Editorial, 17, 56, 57, 60, 74; iStockphoto, 19, 50; Vitoriano Jr./Shutterstock Images, 21; Losevsky Photo and Video/Shutterstock Images, 28; Steve Bower/Shutterstock Images, 32; Falk Kienas/Shutterstock Images, 35; Denis Farrell/AP Images, 39; AP Images, 42, 45; Harvey Georges/AP Images, 48; Francisco Kjolseth/AP Images, 59; Paul Sakuma/AP Images, 61; Chitose Suzuki/AP Images, 65; Denis Bilibouse/AP Images, 67; Toby Talbot/AP Images, 68; iStockphoto/Thinkstock, 72, 94; Solar Systems, HO/AP Images, 81; Timm Schamberger/AP Images, 89; Xu Rupling/AP Images, 97

Library of Congress Cataloging-in-Publication Data
Zuchora-Walske, Christine.
 Solar energy / Christine Zuchora-Walske.
     p. cm. -- (Innovative technologies)
Audience: 11-18.
Includes bibliographical references.
ISBN 978-1-61783-467-7
 1. Solar energy--Juvenile literature. 2. Solar thermal energy--Juvenile literature. I. Title.
TJ810.3.Z83 2013
621.47--dc23
                                         2012024012

TABLE OF CONTENTS

CHAPTER 1
SUN POWER 6

CHAPTER 2
WHY IS SOLAR POWER IMPORTANT? 16

CHAPTER 3
SOLAR THERMAL ENERGY IN HISTORY 30

CHAPTER 4
PHOTOVOLTAIC TECHNOLOGY IN HISTORY 44

CHAPTER 5
SMALL BUT MIGHTY: NANOPHOTOVOLTAICS 52

CHAPTER 6
SQUEEZING SUNLIGHT:
LUMINESCENT SOLAR CONCENTRATORS 70

CHAPTER 7
HEATING THINGS UP:
SOLAR THERMAL INNOVATIONS 78

CHAPTER 8
SOLAR POWER TODAY AND TOMORROW 94

Glossary 102
Additional Resources 104
Source Notes 106
Index 110
About the Author 112
About the Content Consultant 112

CHAPTER 1

SUN POWER

Ever since our solar system began forming approximately 4.6 billion years ago, Earth has been basking in the energy of the sun. But what is the sun? How does it produce energy? And what does that energy do on Earth?

A PORTRAIT OF THE SUN

The sun is a star—a huge ball of incredibly hot gas. It's so big that approximately 1 million Earths could fit inside it.[1] The sun consists of approximately 92 percent hydrogen and 8 percent helium.[2] Gravity holds these gases together, causing great pressure and high temperatures at the sun's core. The core of the sun is approximately 27 million degrees Fahrenheit (15 million°C).[3] That's hot enough for nuclear fusion to happen.

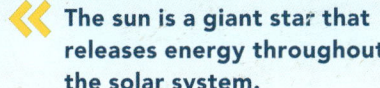
« **The sun is a giant star that releases energy throughout the solar system.**

7

Nuclear fusion is a process that occurs when a substance is so hot its atoms collide at very high speeds, causing them to gain and lose particles. An atom is a basic unit of matter made up of smaller particles called protons, neutrons, and electrons. An atom's nucleus, or center, contains protons and neutrons. A cloud of electrons surrounds the nucleus. When atoms gain or lose particles, they change from one type of substance to another. Inside the sun, the nuclei of hydrogen atoms stick together, and their protons and electrons combine. This process creates helium. It also releases massive amounts of energy. The released energy travels outward from the sun's core. Eventually that energy reaches the rest of the solar system, including Earth.

WHAT IS ENERGY?

Energy exists in all matter. Energy is the ability to change matter or to do work. Work is the force needed to move an object.

Energy takes two main forms:

1. Objects in motion have kinetic energy. So do substances in motion, such as air, and tiny particles in motion, such as molecules and atoms. Sound, heat, light, and electricity come from substances and particles in motion. Therefore, these are types of kinetic energy.
2. Potential energy is the energy matter has because of its position or how its parts are arranged. Potential energy includes elastic and gravitational energy. A slingshot stretched and ready to release a rock is an example of elastic energy. An elevator perched at the top floor of a building has gravitational energy. Its cable is counteracting the pull of Earth's gravity. But if the cable breaks, the elevator will plummet to the bottom of its shaft. It also includes chemical and nuclear energy. Chemical and nuclear energy exist in the bonds that hold together atoms and molecules.

Energy cannot be created or destroyed. It can only change form or location. This change is called energy transfer. Every interaction between things transfers energy.

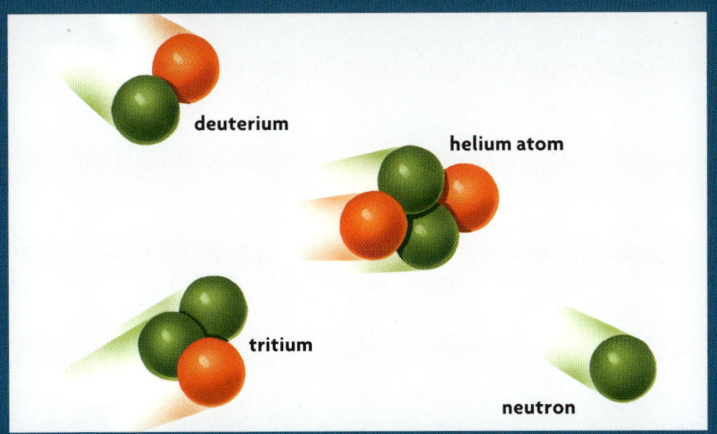

NUCLEAR FUSION

Nuclear fusion means joining smaller nuclei (the plural of nucleus) to make a larger nucleus. Inside the sun, hydrogen atoms undergo nuclear fusion and transform into helium atoms. This process releases huge amounts of heat, light, and other types of energy. In this diagram, two types of hydrogen atoms, deuterium and tritium, undergo fusion, creating a helium atom and an extra particle called a neutron.

SOLAR ENERGY: EARTH'S ENGINE

Earth receives solar energy as light and heat. This light and heat fuels nearly every process that happens on Earth.

For example, sunlight is the first link in every food chain. All plants get the energy they need through photosynthesis. Photosynthesis is a process that changes sunlight into food. A plant absorbs sunlight. The plant also takes in water and carbon dioxide from the air and soil. The energy from sunlight triggers a chemical reaction in the plant. The water and carbon dioxide molecules break up and rearrange into sugar and oxygen molecules. The plant releases the oxygen into the air. It uses the sugar as food so it can grow and function.

The molecules that make up a plant contain chemical energy. Eventually another living thing uses that energy. An herbivore might eat the plant. Digestion releases the plant's chemical energy to help the herbivore grow and function. A carnivore in turn might eat the herbivore. Or it might die and become food for decomposers such as bacteria.

If a plant doesn't get eaten, it might become fuel. For example, a person might burn wood for light and heat. Humans can also process plants to make fuel for machines. Coal, oil, and natural gas are fuels processed by nature. They formed from ancient plant and animal material buried underground. Over millions of years, heat and pressure changed the material into fuels crammed with chemical energy. We call them fossil fuels.

The sun also sets Earth's air and water in motion. As the sun warms our planet's land, oceans, and atmosphere in different amounts at different times and places, it creates ocean currents and weather. Weather refers to conditions in the atmosphere such as temperature, wind, and rainfall or snowfall. By moving air and water around, the sun makes wind power and hydropower possible.

USING THE SUN

Humans use the sun's energy indirectly in many ways. We can use the sun's energy directly, too. All solar technologies fall into two main categories: photovoltaic and solar thermal.

A photovoltaic cell, or solar cell, converts sunlight directly to electricity. Solar cells mostly consist of semiconductors. Semiconductors are materials that conduct electricity in a way that can be controlled. Dozens of natural elements—and compounds of multiple elements—are semiconductors. The most common photovoltaic semiconductor is silicon, a type of crystal.

Semiconductors absorb solar energy as they are hit by the sun. The solar energy hits the atoms in the semiconductor, freeing some electrons from the atoms. The atomic structure of semiconductors forces the electrons to flow in one direction. The movement of the electrons is what makes the electric current.

DOPING SILICON

The type of silicon most commonly used in solar cells is monocrystalline silicon. In this form of silicon, the silicon atoms bond to one another to form a structure with a uniform pattern called a lattice. The lattice forms when each electron bonds with an electron from another atom.

In pure monocrystalline silicon, almost every electron is bonded to another one. There aren't many loners, so sunlight hitting the lattice does not free many electrons. In other words, pure silicon is a poor conductor of electricity.

But scientists discovered they could dope silicon, or mix in a tiny amount of some other material, to make the silicon a better conductor. The added material is called an impurity. This type of impurity isn't a bad thing; it simply means the crystal is no longer made purely of silicon.

Doping changes the crystal lattice by inserting non-silicon atoms here and there and creating more loner electrons. So when sunlight hits the doped silicon, it can free more electrons—and those electrons will move in only one direction. When manufacturers process silicon for use in solar cells, they can control its conductivity by manipulating the type and amount of impurities they use in doping.

A group of linked solar cells is called a solar module. Solar modules can be part of huge arrays or small enough to power electronic devices. Perhaps the most familiar use is the rooftop solar modules commonly found on houses.

Solar thermal technology harnesses the heat of sunlight. For example, people can engineer their buildings to make the most of sunlight's warmth. This technique is called passive solar building design. We can also use sunlight to either boil water or heat a gas to spin a turbine, which then generates electricity. This process happens in a solar thermal power plant.

A solar thermal power plant such as this power tower system uses sunlight to boil oil to create usable energy.

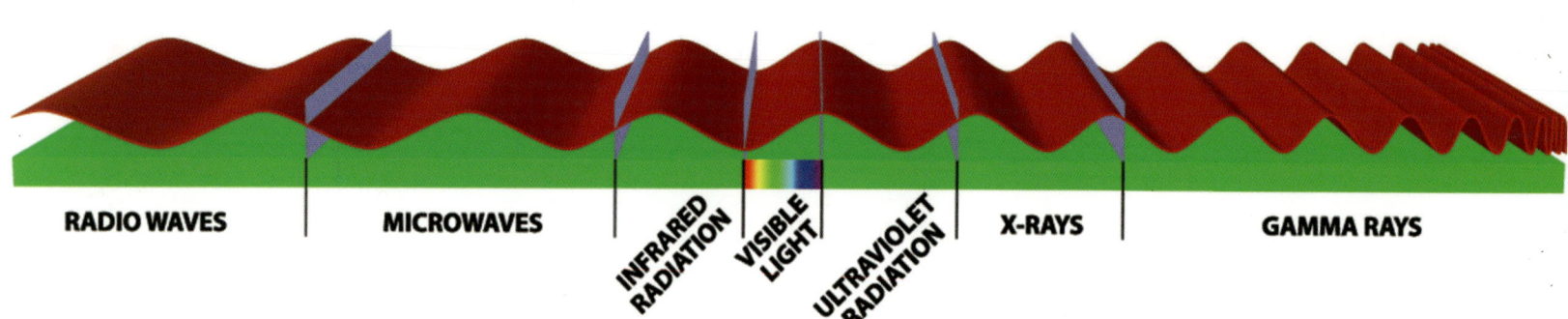

THE SOLAR SPECTRUM «

Solar energy travels as radiation. That means it travels in rays (straight lines) outward in all directions. Solar energy travels along the rays in the form of a wave. We call it a wave because the energy alternates between higher and lower values, like a water wave. Wavelength is the distance between two successive wave crests. Frequency is how many crests pass a given point every second.

The sun emits energy in a range of wavelengths. The full range is called the solar spectrum. The sun emits a small amount of radio waves and microwaves (longest wavelengths). Most solar radiation is (from longer to shorter wavelengths) infrared, visible, or ultraviolet. The sun also emits a small amount of X-rays and gamma rays (shortest wavelength).

Our senses can detect only some types of solar radiation. Nerve cells in our skin detect infrared radiation as heat. Nerve cells in our eyes detect visible light as a variety of colors. Our bodies cannot detect radio waves, microwaves, ultraviolet radiation, X-rays, or gamma rays.

CHAPTER 2

WHY IS SOLAR POWER IMPORTANT?

The United States, similar to many other industrialized nations, is hooked on fossil fuels. But coal, oil, and natural gas are problematic energy sources for a variety of social, economic, and security reasons. Many people believe we need to change our energy habits to include more sustainable or green energy sources, including solar energy.

OUR ENERGY HABITS

The United States uses a lot of energy. It is home to approximately 5 percent of the world's population. Meanwhile, it consumes approximately 20 percent of the world's energy.[1] Americans use fossil fuels for approximately 83 percent of their energy needs.[2]

Generating electricity is one key use of fossil fuels in the United States. Coal is the most common fuel source for this purpose. In 2011, approximately 42 percent of

« **The United States is greatly dependent on fossil fuels for everyday life.**

> ### WHAT IS GREEN ENERGY?
>
> Green energy is energy that creates little or no pollution and comes from renewable resources. Renewable resources are ones that nature can replace. Green energy includes a wide range of technologies, such as solar power, wind power, biofuels, hydroelectricity, and geothermal energy. Some people also consider nuclear power to be green energy because it is cleaner than fossil fuels.

electricity generated in the United States came from coal-fired turbines. Natural gas is another important fuel source. In 2011, approximately 25 percent of electricity generated in the United States came from natural gas–fired turbines. Approximately 1 percent of our electricity came from burning oil. That means fossil fuels were responsible for approximately 68 percent of US electricity. Another 19 percent came from nuclear power and 13 percent from renewable sources, such as hydropower, wind power, and solar power. Renewable sources increased 3 percent from 2010.[3]

Transportation is another major use of fossil fuels in the United States. Most US vehicles—automobiles, boats, trains, airplanes, and more—run on fuels made from oil. Even vehicles that use electricity get that electricity mostly from burning fossil fuels. In fact, of all the oil used in the United States in 2010, approximately 70 percent went to transportation purposes, such as gasoline, diesel fuel, jet fuel, and asphalt roads.[4]

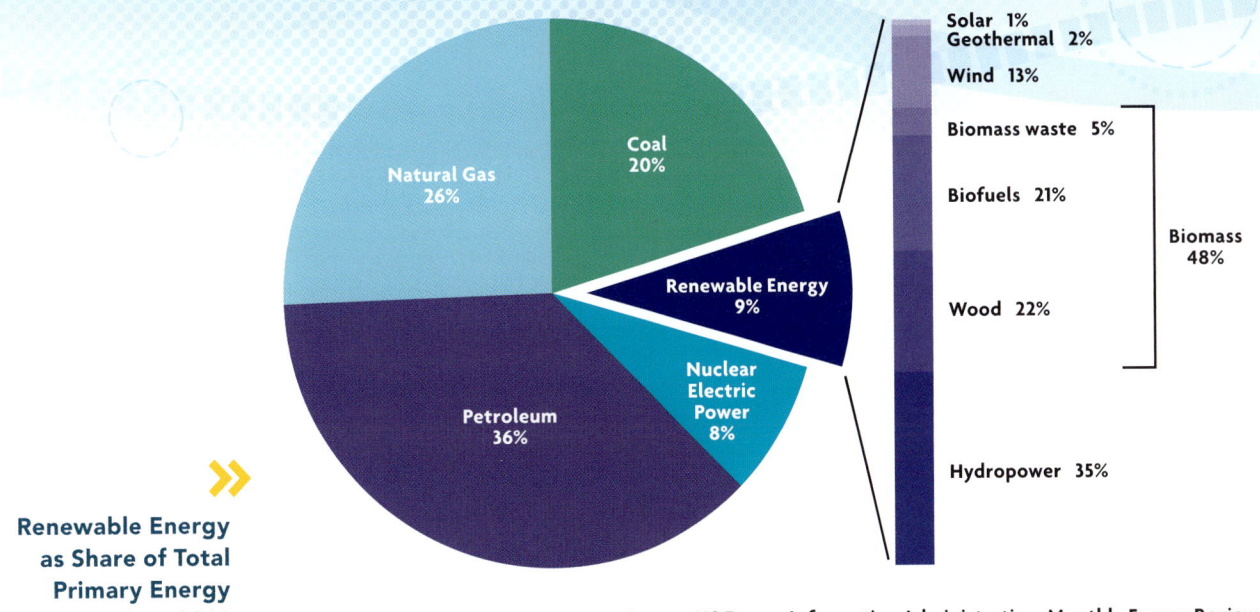

Renewable Energy as Share of Total Primary Energy Consumption, 2011

Source: US Energy Information Administration, Monthly Energy Review

Heating and cooling are also key uses of fossil fuels in the United States. In parts of the nation that have harsh winters or sweltering summers, homes and businesses rely on natural gas and oil—or electricity generated largely by fossil fuels—to keep their buildings at a safe and comfortable temperature.

THE FOSSIL FUEL DILEMMA

Americans have logical reasons for using so much energy. The United States has the largest economy in the world, and that economy is energy intensive. Furthermore, residents of the United States are accustomed to high technology and a high level of comfort and convenience in their daily lives. Maintaining that quality of life requires a lot of energy.

US residents rely heavily on fossil fuels for a few practical reasons. One important reason is that fossil fuels pack a huge energy punch. Coal, oil, and natural gas are crammed with stored chemical energy. Another key reason is the relatively low cost of fossil fuels. Right now, coal, oil, and natural gas are plentiful around the world, and energy infrastructure—including mines, wells, refineries, power plants, transmission lines, pipelines, and gas stations—is built around them. That means the monetary cost of extracting, processing, and distributing fossil fuels is lower than the cost of developing and distributing energy from renewable sources.

But fossil fuels have serious drawbacks, too. They are nonrenewable. A nonrenewable energy source is one that can't be replenished in a short period of time. Fossil fuels took millions of years and special, extreme conditions to form. We cannot expect our planet to form any more fossil fuels.

One unfortunate risk of fossil fuel use is oil spills that can harm animals, plants, and their habitats.

Another drawback of heavy fossil fuel use is that it forces the United States to depend on other nations for energy. There's plenty of coal and natural gas in North America. But approximately half of US oil is imported. The price or the supply of imported oil can fluctuate. Because the country needs a steady, ample flow of oil—especially for transportation—a rise in price or a disruption in supply drags down its economy. US dependence on imported oil complicates international relations too. When the US government deals with countries that sell oil, it must carefully consider the effect those dealings might have on the supply of imported oil.

Many people believe fossil fuels' most troubling drawback is their impact on the environment. All three fuels have negative effects at each step along the path from extraction to burning. For example, coal mining may destroy landscapes, pollute streams, and sicken or even kill miners. Oil drilling and distribution by pipeline or vehicle can cause oil spills that kill wildlife and contaminate soil and water. Natural gas drilling, too, can contaminate water both above and below Earth's surface. Burning fossil fuels produces a variety of toxic emissions, including as carbon monoxide, sulfur dioxide, and tiny particles that contribute to acid rain, smog, respiratory illnesses, and lung disease.

In addition to toxic emissions, the burning of fossil fuels also releases carbon dioxide (CO_2) into Earth's atmosphere. CO_2 is a greenhouse gas. The more greenhouse gases Earth's

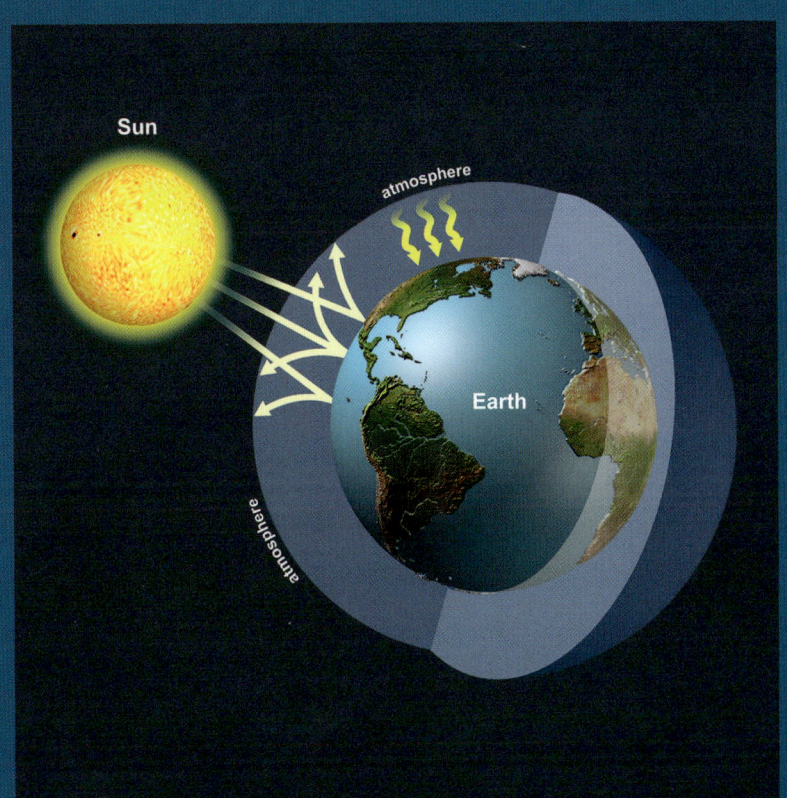

THE GREENHOUSE EFFECT

Earth and its atmosphere work somewhat like a greenhouse. Sunlight passes easily through the panes of glass into the greenhouse. The sunlight warms the objects inside the greenhouse. The warm objects radiate heat. But that heat can't escape the greenhouse, so the temperature inside the greenhouse rises.

Similarly, sunlight passes easily through Earth's atmosphere to Earth. Snow, ice, and clouds reflect some of this solar energy back out to space. But land, water, trees, buildings, and other objects absorb lots of solar energy. As they do so, Earth's surface warms up. The warm surface radiates heat. Some of this heat escapes directly to space. But greenhouse gases absorb some of the heat. These gases reradiate the heat they absorb again and again. The overall effect is to trap heat in Earth's atmosphere. This heat-trapping process is called the greenhouse effect.

atmosphere contains, the more heat the atmosphere traps. Many scientists agree that atmospheric CO_2 is rising and that Earth's average temperature is rising with the CO_2. This rise is called climate change or global warming. The average temperature of Earth's surface has

CLIMATE CHANGE CHAIN REACTION

Small changes in temperature can cause big chain reactions. For example, Earth's polar ice caps are beginning to melt. Polar ice contains a lot of water. Depending on how much ice melts, it could raise the sea level from a few inches to many feet. Sea level rise could flood coastal areas around the world, endangering the people living there. Ice reflects a lot of solar energy back into space. When ice melts, it exposes the land or water beneath it. Land and water absorb more heat, which causes more warming, more melting, and more rising sea levels. Polar ice is frozen freshwater. Large quantities of freshwater melting into the ocean could disturb deep ocean currents. Deep ocean currents swirl around the continents in a predictable way, carrying heat and helping determine weather. If ocean currents change, they could disrupt normal weather patterns. Places that usually get moderate rain could have droughts or floods. The timing of seasons may change. Plants and animals that can't adjust to the changes may die out. People may find they can no longer grow the crops they're used to growing. The chain reactions go on and on.

risen approximately 1.4 degrees Fahrenheit (0.8°C) over the past century.[5] That may seem like a small change—but it's actually a big problem. Climate change is wreaking havoc on Earth's environment.

No one knows for sure how conditions on Earth might change as a result of accumulating greenhouse gases and rising temperatures. But most scientists agree climate changes are already under way, and many predict dramatic changes in the future. They recommend people prepare for such changes, try to adapt to them, and try to slow the pace of climate change by reducing greenhouse gas emissions into the atmosphere—especially CO_2. They say conserving energy isn't enough. To prevent severe climate change, people must switch to energy sources that don't release greenhouse gases.

Many people believe it's time for the United States—and the world—to invest in and develop renewable energy seriously. Green energy can lead to a cleaner, safer, healthier future for Earth and all its inhabitants.

SOLAR POWER: PART OF THE SOLUTION

Humankind's response to the fossil fuel dilemma will need to be as sophisticated as the problem is complicated. It will need to include many different sources of green energy and many different approaches to developing these sources. Solar power is just one important part of that response.

The sun is a plentiful source of clean, renewable energy. Each year the sun gives Earth's surface ten times as much energy as is stored in all the world's reserves of coal and oil. And it won't run out in the foreseeable future. As long as the sun continues to burn, it will radiate energy. Scientists expect the sun to keep providing a life-sustaining level of energy to Earth for approximately 5 billion years. Solar energy releases no chemical pollution into the air, water, or soil. Nor does it add greenhouse gases to the atmosphere. Moreover, sunlight is free and accessible everywhere on Earth. No single person or nation controls solar energy, and it doesn't need to be extracted, transported, or bought.

But solar energy isn't a perfect solution to our planet's energy problems. It, like any source of energy, has limitations and faces challenges.

One key challenge is cost. While sunlight itself is free, the technology needed to convert sunlight into electricity or to harness its heat is expensive. The cost of manufacturing and installing photovoltaic and solar thermal systems—as well as the infrastructure needed to distribute electricity from solar power plants—is high compared to the cost of extracting and distributing fossil fuels with an infrastructure that's already built and paid for. Solar power can't yet compete.

And while solar technology does not pollute, it does affect Earth's ecosystems. Solar power stations take up large areas of land, and many people find them ugly. Many people find smaller solar installations awkward and ugly, too. The silicon and other minerals used to make photovoltaic cells must be mined. Both the mining process and the construction of large solar arrays can upset nature's beauty and its delicate balance.

Finally, while the sun shines all over the Earth, it doesn't shine equally everywhere all the time. A solar facility in a spot that gets full sun year-round will produce steady, reliable power. But a facility in a place with unpredictable sunlight will produce smaller, less predictable amounts of solar power.

LOW-TECH INNOVATIONS

High technology isn't the only way to make good use of solar energy in the modern world. Simpler technology can be just as important. In some parts of the world, organizations are distributing solar cookers to help people cook their food in a safer, cheaper, more environmentally friendly way.

In one example, in 2005, approximately 17,000 people were living in the Iridimi refugee camp in eastern Chad. These people, who fled the war-torn Darfur region of Sudan, traditionally used firewood for cooking. But wood was scarce in Iridimi and throughout Chad, which is mostly desert, so women and girls had to travel far outside the camp to find it. Many of them suffered violent attacks from rebel soldiers, bandits, and local villagers who didn't want to share their few resources. Cooking fires caused many burns and breathing problems. Wood-based cooking contributed to deforestation. And ironically, it increased malnutrition. Families often got wood by bartering some of their food, which left them with less to eat. They also avoided eating protein-rich foods such as beans because cooking them used up too much wood.

Aid organizations began providing thousands of low-cost solar cookers to the Iridimi refugees. These cookers were made of cardboard and aluminum foil folded into a basket shape, with a specially designed cooking pot resting in the center. Everyone used the cookers. People ate more and better food. Health, safety, and air quality improved. Trips outside the camp dropped 86 percent, and violent attacks virtually disappeared.[6]

Many scientists, inventors, and entrepreneurs are looking for ways to overcome these limitations. They believe it's high time we made the most of the sun—as part of a larger shift away from fossil fuels and toward green energy. These innovators are the latest in a long line of people who have created solar technologies throughout human history.

« **Solar panels can produce power only when the sun is shining.**

CHAPTER 3

SOLAR THERMAL ENERGY IN HISTORY

For as long as humans have existed, we have used the sun's energy to serve our daily needs. Throughout the centuries, people have kept coming up with new and clever solar technologies. Solar thermal technology has been around for thousands of years.

ANCIENT SOLAR TECHNOLOGIES

As early as the seventh century, people used glass lenses or reflective materials such as polished metal to concentrate the sun's rays into an intensely hot and bright beam of light. This beam of light could then start a fire.

Ancient people used these lenses for both practical and ceremonial purposes. They could start a fire for cooking or warmth, or they could use the fire as a medical treatment. For example, the ancient Greeks used burning glasses to close wounds.

« We have long used lenses to create fire using sunlight.

31

The ancient Greeks, Romans, and Chinese all used burning mirrors to light sacred fires in holy places such as temples. Anthemius of Tralles, a Greek mathematician, wrote a treatise titled "On Burning Mirrors." This document explained how people could use mirrors to blind or burn their enemies.

"It is pleasant to have one's house cool in summer and warm in winter, is it not? . . . Now, supposing a house to have a southern aspect, sunshine during winter will steal in under the verandah, but in summer, when the sun traverses a path right over our heads, the roof will afford an agreeable shade, will it not? If, then, such an arrangement is desirable, the southern side of a house should be built higher to catch the rays of the winter sun, and the northern side lower to prevent the cold winds finding ingress."[1] **—Greek philosopher Socrates (469–399 BCE)**

All these examples show ancient humans understood that sunlight contains a lot of energy. And they understood they could capture, concentrate, and focus that energy for either constructive or destructive uses.

Ancient people also understood they could engineer their homes and other structures to maximize or minimize the warmth of sunlight. Today, this technique is called passive solar building design. For example, the Greeks built their houses facing south to keep them cool in summer and warm in winter. They knew that in their part of the world, the sun would be high overhead in the summer and wouldn't shine into south-facing doors and windows. In winter, however, the sun would be lower in the southern sky and would shine in, providing welcome warmth. The Romans used similar principles when they built public bathhouses with huge south-facing windows.

Passive solar building design remained important in Europe all the way through the Middle Ages (500s–1500s CE). In fact, it was so important that the Justinian Code included a section ensuring individual access to sunlight. The Justinian Code is a collection of laws in force during the Byzantine Empire (330–1453).

Throughout the Middle Ages, people continued to use burning mirrors in ways similar to those ancient people had used. For example, metalworkers often used burning mirrors to melt solder, a metal used to join two pieces of another kind of metal. And military strategists kept dreaming up ideas for using burning mirrors as weapons. One medieval drawing shows a lighthouse using a large burning mirror to set a ship aflame.

On the other side of the world, the Anasazi people of southwestern North America used passive solar building design too. From approximately 1100 to 1300, they built compact cities into cliff sides. The buildings typically opened to the south, which helped them receive as much

sunlight as possible in the winter and helped keep them cool in the summer. The backs of the buildings snuggled into the cliffs, which protected them from the summer sun and the winter's cold.

RENAISSANCE AND EARLY MODERN ADVANCES

In the early sixteenth century, Italian scientist, artist, and writer Leonardo da Vinci suggested a completely new way for people to use burning mirrors. From 1513 to 1516, he sketched and wrote about his idea for a huge mirror meant to heat substances in large quantities for industrial use. The curved, circular mirror would be approximately four miles (6 km) wide.[2] It would be made of many smaller mirrors set in a shallow basin dug into the ground. All the mirrors would reflect sunlight onto a tall pole in the center. The pole would hold a tank full of material to be heated, such as water for boiling or metal for melting.

A century later, French engineer Salomon de Caux built the first mechanical device powered by solar thermal energy. The device was made of a supporting frame, glass lenses, and a sealed metal vessel containing air and water. The lenses focused sunlight onto the vessel. This heated up the air inside, which then expanded. The expanding air pushed on the water, producing a small water fountain.

« **The Anasazi site Cliff Palace in Mesa Verde National Park is one example of passive solar building.**

In the 1700s, Swiss physicist Horace-Bénédict de Saussure noticed, like many people before him, that "a room, a carriage, or any other place is hotter when the rays of the sun pass through glass."[3] He wondered just how hot it could get inside a glass solar heat trap, or "hot box." In 1767, he decided to find out. Through a series of experiments, he eventually created a hot box that reached an inner temperature of 228 degrees Fahrenheit (108°C)—hot enough to boil water and cook food.

Later scientists built upon Saussure's work to construct solar cookers. For example, in the 1830s, British astronomer John Herschel traveled to South Africa to study the skies of the Southern Hemisphere. He did a lot of other things, too—including experimenting with hot boxes. Herschel built one that heated its contents to 240 degrees Fahrenheit (116°C).[4] To his companions' delight, he demonstrated that it could cook meat, boil eggs, and make stews.

SOLAR ENGINES AND WATER HEATERS

Augustin Mouchot was a French mathematician. In 1860, he began experimenting with solar thermal energy. Building on the work of his predecessors, he designed a solar oven, a solar still (which he used to distill wine into brandy), and a solar fountain. But he believed these were just novelties. He really wanted to use solar energy for powering the most important technology of his day, the steam engine. He believed humans would eventually use up the coal that fired most

A man from Zanskar, India, uses a solar cooker to cook food for himself and his family—a modern take on Herschel's ideas.

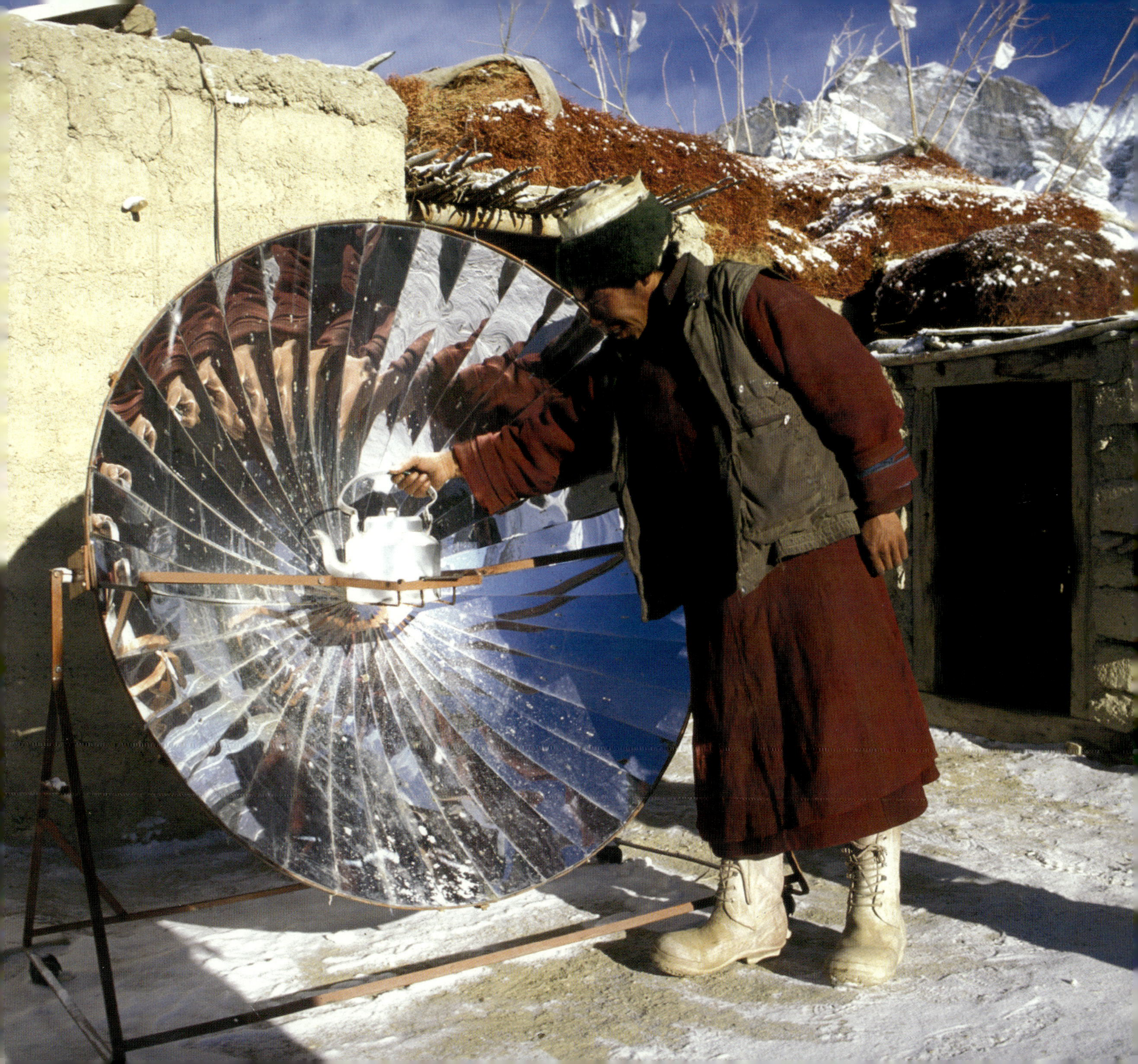

of the world's steam engines. And he saw that coal was not universally accessible, while sunlight was. He wanted to develop an alternative to coal-fired steam engines—and in 1866, he finally succeeded. He designed the first solar-powered steam engine. He used mirrors to focus sunlight on a glass-encased iron cauldron filled with water. The heat caused the water to boil, which created steam to power a steam engine.

The scientific community and the public praised Mouchot's accomplishment. Over the next few decades, he and several other scientists refined the technology and applied solar engines to a variety of uses, such as running printing presses and pumping water. But by the early 1900s, businesses and governments were losing interest in solar engines. Humans were finding more and more coal around the world, and mining methods were improving rapidly. Coal had become abundant and cheap, and thousands of factories were already outfitted with coal-fired steam engines. Solar engines simply couldn't compete.

HOW A STEAM ENGINE WORKS

A steam engine has six basic parts:

1. an external heat source
2. a boiler full of water
3. a valve
4. a cylinder
5. a piston
6. a wheel

The heat source, such as a coal fire or concentrated sunlight, heats the water inside the boiler. When the water gets hot enough, it becomes steam, and its volume increases 1,600 times. The expanding steam presses against the inside of the boiler and escapes with great force through the valve into the cylinder. Inside the cylinder, the moving steam pushes a piston back and forth. The piston's rod is connected by a crank to a wheel, which converts the piston's back-and-forth movement into a rotating motion.

While interest in solar engines was fading, solar water heaters were growing more popular—especially in the southern and western United States. From approximately 1890 to 1920, Americans bought tens of thousands of solar water heaters. At that time, solar water heating was far cheaper and easier than heating water with wood, coal, oil, gas, or electricity.

The earliest solar water heaters were simple metal tanks painted black to absorb as much sunlight as possible. Black objects absorb more sunlight than light-colored objects. These tanks heated water slowly and cooled quickly at night, so engineers kept tinkering to improve the design. By the 1920s, the best solar water heater was one that had two main parts: a heating element exposed to the sun and an insulated storage tank inside the house. The heating element consisted of many pipes attached to a black metal sheet inside a glass-covered

HOW A TURBINE GENERATES ELECTRICITY

A turbine has three main parts: a rotor, a shaft, and a generator. The rotor looks like a fan with many blades. The blades are attached to a central piece called a hub. As steam pushes against the blades, they move. This movement makes the hub spin. Alternatively, an engine can spin the rotor. The hub is attached to a rod called the shaft. As the hub spins, so does the shaft. The spinning shaft is attached to an electric generator. The generator contains a set of strong magnets and coils of metal wire. As the shaft spins the magnets inside the generator, they push electrons through the wire. The flowing electrons create an electric current within the wire.

box. This element was usually on the roof. The water heated quickly because it passed in small volumes through narrow pipes instead of sitting in one big tank. And when stored in an insulated indoor tank, the water stayed hot overnight.

After 1920, solar water heaters waned in popularity. By this time, oil companies were extracting large quantities of oil and natural gas from deposits around the world. As these fossil fuels became more plentiful, they also got cheaper.

FIGHTING RISING ENERGY COSTS

In the 1940s, passive solar construction enjoyed a resurgence in the United States. World War II (1939–1945) took a huge bite out of the US fossil fuel supply. Heating fuel was scarce, so passive solar homes and buildings were in great demand.

For nearly three decades after World War II, fossil fuel usage soared. These fuels had become the industrial world's key sources of energy. The United States, a huge energy user, had plenty of its own coal. But it grew dependent on foreign countries for oil.

The Arab nations of the Middle East were the world's biggest oil suppliers. These nations opposed many US policies. Arab nations especially disliked the US alliance with Israel, a country most Arab nations considered an enemy. When the United States supported Israel's military

In the twenty-first century, solar water heaters are being embraced again in less developed countries including South Africa.

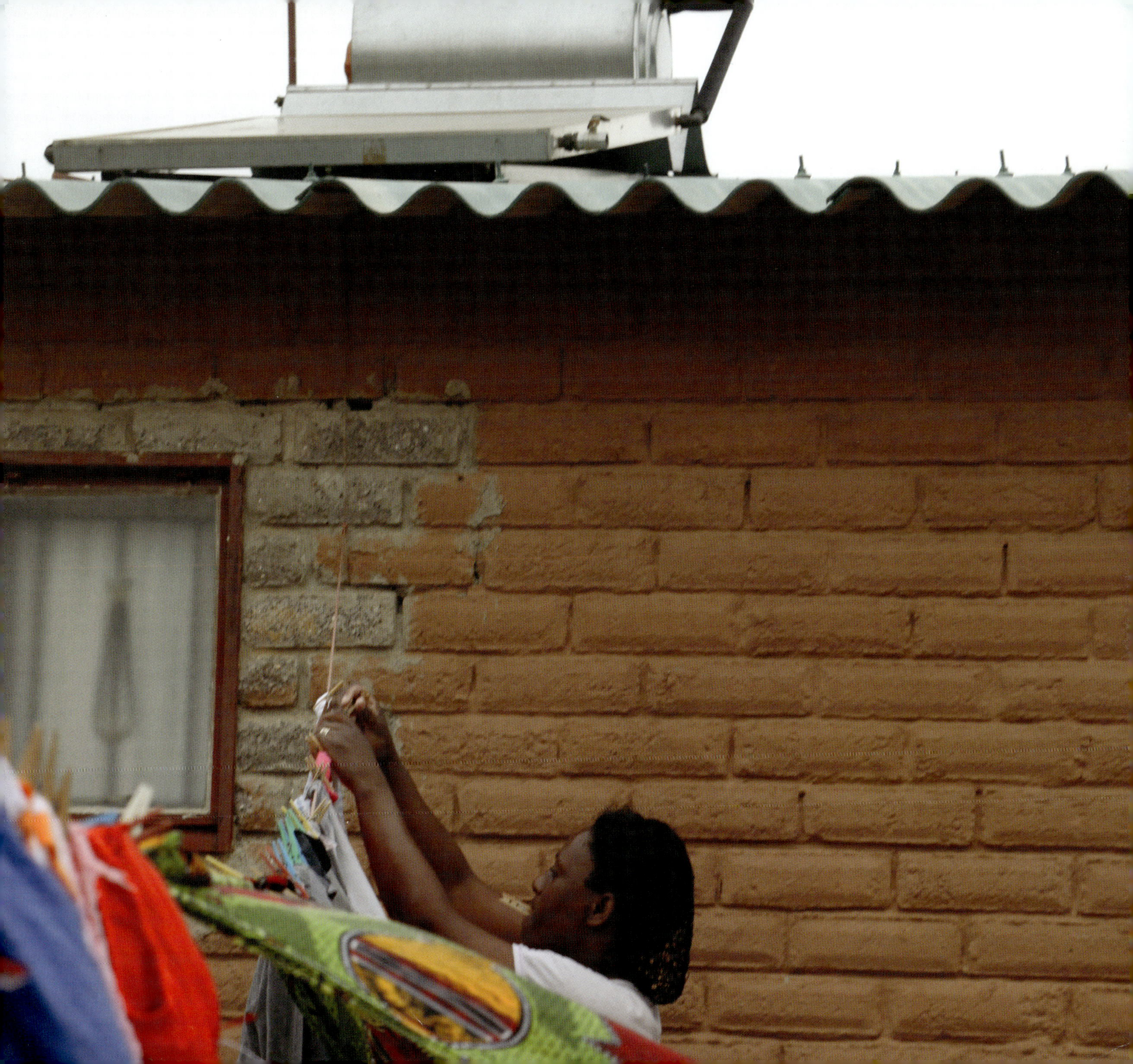

HOOKED ON FOSSIL FUELS

The steam engine was invented in the mid-eighteenth century. Before long, it was powering machinery around the globe. It burned coal, because no other widely available fuel provided as much energy. People eventually used coal for heating and powering electrical generators, too. For approximately two centuries, coal was the king of fuels.

In the late nineteenth century, inventors perfected the internal combustion engine (ICE). They found that gasoline, which is made from oil, was the ICE's perfect fuel, and that the ICE was a perfect engine for the automobile. By the late 1920s, millions of automobiles had rolled off assembly lines. Huge oil companies formed to supply gasoline for all these vehicles. Within a few decades, oil became a crucial resource.

In the twenty-first century, industrial nations still rely heavily on fossil fuels such as coal, oil, and natural gas. Factories and power plants are the main users of coal and natural gas. Oil is the world's primary transportation fuel.

in a 1973 war against several Arab nations, Arab leaders got angry. They retaliated against the United States by slowing the flow of oil to a trickle. The Organization of Arab Petroleum Exporting Countries (OAPEC) raised oil prices by 70 percent.[5] It also began reducing oil production 5 percent per month.[6]

As a result of this oil embargo, gasoline became very scarce and expensive for Americans. The embargo ended in 1974, but another energy crisis occurred in 1979. More and more people supported energy conservation, renewable energy, and energy independence. US leaders started developing alternative energy sources, including solar energy.

The United States, Spain, Israel, and a few other countries built experimental solar thermal power plants. A solar thermal power plant uses sunlight as a heat source to either boil water or heat a gas and spin a turbine, which then generates electricity.

By the 1990s, many solar thermal power plants had been built around the world. But as prices for oil and natural gas fell, the solar thermal industry stalled. In the meantime, photovoltaic technology took over the solar industry.

WORLD'S FIRST SUN POWERED AUTOMOBILE
INTERNATIONAL RECTIFIER
CORPORATION
CALIFORNIA
HORSELESS CARRIAGE 2103
YVB 65

CHAPTER 4

PHOTOVOLTAIC TECHNOLOGY IN HISTORY

Photovoltaic technology is much younger than solar thermal technology. But it's not as new as many people think. It's been around for nearly two centuries.

THE FIRST PHOTOVOLTAICS

French physicist Alexandre-Edmond Becquerel discovered photovoltaics in 1839. While conducting experiments with metal electrodes placed in liquids, Becquerel found that exposure to sunlight increased the flow of electrons.

In 1876, British scientist William Grylls Adams and his student, Richard Evans Day, discovered that sunlight produces an electrical current within the mineral selenium. Seven years later, US inventor Charles Fritts made the first solar cell. It was a coin-sized wafer of selenium coated with a transparent gold film. Fritts's solar cell had an

« In 1960, Dr. Charles Escoffery toured Europe in what was believed to be the first solar-powered car.

45

> **PHOTOVOLTAIC EFFICIENCY**
>
> Sunlight is made up of many different wavelengths, each of which has a different energy level. Only certain wavelengths, or energy levels, can create an electric current when they hit a solar cell. The percentage of energy a solar cell converts into electricity from the sunlight that hits it is called its efficiency. The most advanced solar cells have an efficiency of approximately 40 percent.[2] But most solar cells capture less than 20 percent of the energy that strikes them.[3]

efficiency of 1 percent.[1] That means it converted approximately 1 percent of the sunlight hitting it into electricity.

It took 70 years for researchers to develop solar cells people could use for practical purposes. In 1953, Gerald Pearson, a physicist at Bell Laboratories, accidentally created a silicon solar cell. The silicon cell was several times more efficient than a selenium one. Two other Bell scientists, Daryl Chapin and Calvin Fuller, refined Pearson's solar cell. In 1954, they created the first photovoltaic cell that produced enough electricity to power ordinary electrical devices.

At first, solar cells were extremely expensive to make. Their high cost meant electric power providers were not interested in installing them to generate power. And most electronics manufacturers weren't interested, either. Only toy makers used them for novelty items such as miniature vehicles and beach radios.

>> **Scientists in the 1950s and 1960s were excited to put solar cells on satellites.**

In the late 1950s, a group of scientists lobbied the US Navy to install solar cells as a power source for Vanguard I, the second artificial US satellite. Although the navy was skeptical of the new technology, it agreed to supplement Vanguard's chemical batteries with solar cells. This fateful decision gave solar cells a chance to prove themselves. About a week after the Vanguard's 1958 launch, the chemical batteries failed. The solar cells, however, worked for years. Solar cells became the standard energy source for spacecraft of all kinds.

Throughout the 1960s, researchers continued to refine photovoltaic technology. The efficiency of solar cells increased. Engineers linked the cells together to form modules. But photovoltaics were still expensive, and few industries used them.

BECOMING COST EFFECTIVE

In 1968, a chemist named Elliot Berman set out to develop a cheaper solar cell. He figured that if he could lower the price, photovoltaic technology would become popular in remote places that needed electricity. Berman was right. In the early 1970s, he created successful solar modules with lower-grade materials, thus slashing the price of solar energy.

"The primary criteria for any terrestrial power device, Berman knew, 'is how many kilowatt-hours you get for a dollar.'"[4]—**Author John Perlin**

Oil and gas companies were the first major buyers of solar modules for use on Earth. Offshore oil rigs and remote gas and oil fields needed electricity for their lights, wells, and other equipment. They had been using huge chemical batteries, but these were bulky, toxic, and short lived. Solar modules provided a smaller, cleaner, cheaper, and longer-lasting alternative.

Purchases from the petroleum industry gave the photovoltaic industry the cash it needed to survive and evolve. Soon the US Coast Guard followed the oil and gas companies' lead and began using solar modules to power lighthouses and buoys. US railroads came right behind them, installing solar devices to run signaling equipment along the nation's railways.

In 1977, the US Department of Energy established the National Renewable Energy Laboratory, a federal facility devoted to harnessing power from the sun. With both industrial and governmental support, the pace of photovoltaic development and use increased through the 1980s and 1990s.

In 2012, public policy researchers at the University of Tennessee published a study examining the effect of federal incentives on emerging energy technologies, including solar energy. Researchers found that it typically takes any energy technology approximately 30 years to reach widespread adoption.[5] Federal incentives have been vital to developing fossil fuel technologies and nuclear power—and they are just as important for developing solar and other green energy technologies. Government support removes barriers and encourages private investment.

Today, small solar modules power a dizzying array of devices, from cellular phones to parking meters. Photovoltaic cells integrated into construction materials—such as roofing,

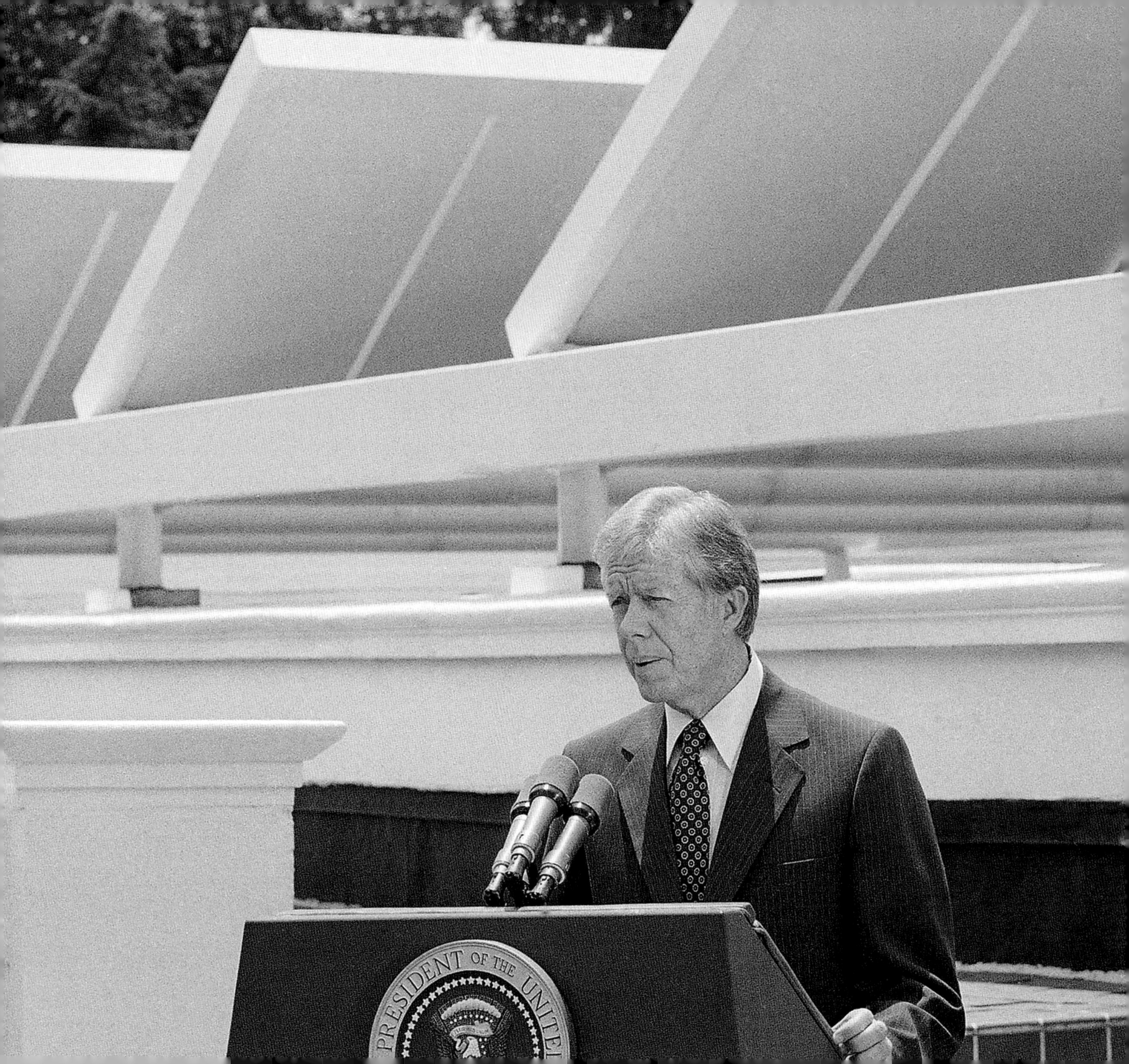
PRESIDENT OF THE UNITED

siding, skylights, windows, and facades—help homes and buildings generate electricity without bulky solar panels. Solar cells with special structures at the microscopic level boost the cells' efficiency. Thanks to these and other astounding innovations—both photovoltaic and solar thermal—solar energy holds more promise for humankind than ever.

> **WHITE HOUSE SOLAR PANELS**
>
> President Jimmy Carter was a strong supporter of solar energy development. During his administration, the White House was partially solar powered. On June 20, 1979, the Carter administration installed 32 solar panels on the roof of the White House. These panels harvested sunlight to heat water used in the White House.
>
> In 1986 the administration of Carter's successor, Ronald Reagan, dismantled the White House solar panels while resurfacing the roof. By then, the Reagan administration had also cut the US Department of Energy budget for research and development of renewable energy and eliminated tax breaks for installing wind turbines and solar technologies. This act set back solar development temporarily.

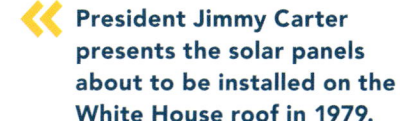

« **President Jimmy Carter presents the solar panels about to be installed on the White House roof in 1979.**

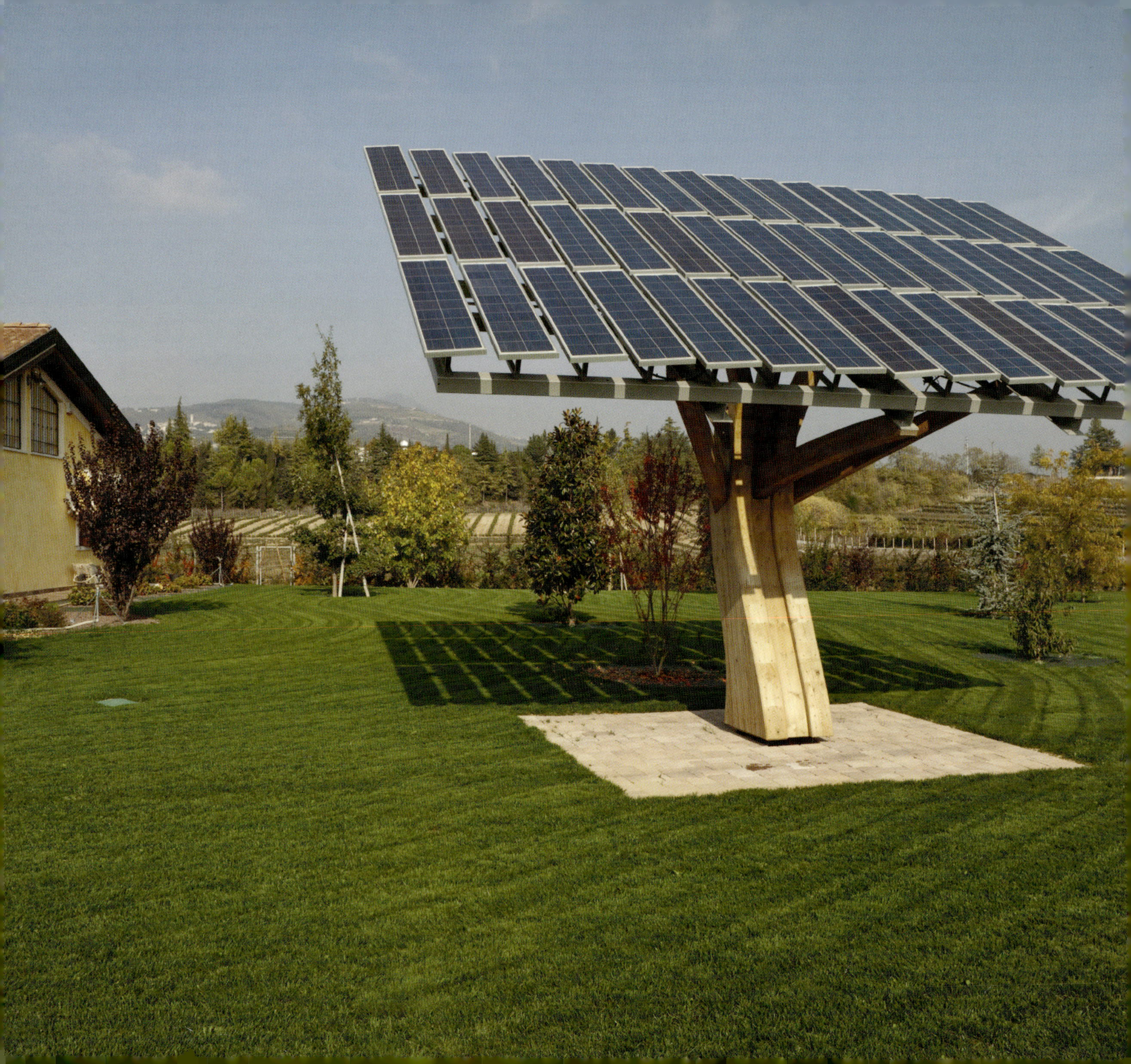

CHAPTER 5

SMALL BUT MIGHTY: NANOPHOTOVOLTAICS

People have been using solar cells for more than a half-century. They're an obvious choice for spacecraft, small electronics, and remote or sunny locations. The sun is a clean, free, and never-ending source of power, and photovoltaic science is well understood. But surprisingly, we don't use solar cells for everything. We don't even use them for most things. But why?

A few key issues have prevented widespread use of photovoltaic technology. Some of its most problematic limitations are the efficiency, size, and cost of solar modules.

Let's say a solar cell is 15 percent efficient. That means it converts only 15 percent of the sunlight hitting it into electricity. To gain more energy to power a device, designers must keep adding solar cells until together they generate enough power to run the device. But more solar cells may present a new set of problems. Adding solar cells can

« **Some people dislike the bulk and appearance of traditional solar panels.**

THE COST OF SOLAR CELLS

Why are solar cells so expensive? "The problem with traditional solar cells," says Brandon MacDonald, a researcher at Australia's University of Melbourne, "is that making them requires many complex and energy-intensive steps."[1]

Most solar cells in use today are traditional solar cells made of crystalline silicon. Converting raw silicon into photovoltaic cells is an arduous and costly process. It must occur under vacuum conditions and be heated in special kilns to 2,552 degrees Fahrenheit (1,400°C).

Moreover, silicon is plentiful on Earth, but it's also in high demand. The photovoltaic industry needs silicon for solar cells, and the electronics industry uses silicon for computer chips. Competition between these two industries for a limited supply encourages silicon producers to raise their prices.

increase the weight, size, and cost of a device to a point where it's too big, heavy, or awkward to operate; too bulky and unsightly to appeal to consumers; or too expensive for the people who might want to buy it.

Some researchers are using nanoscience to overcome these limitations. Nanoscience is the study of extremely small things, or things in nanoscale—between 1 to 100 nanometers. A nanometer is so small that it takes 10 million nanometers to make 1 centimeter, or 25.4 million nanometers to make 1 inch. Scientists can apply nanotechnology, including nanoscale methods and tools, to photovoltaics in a variety of ways.

THIN-FILM SOLAR CELLS

Thin-film solar cells are one important type of nanophotovoltaics. Manufacturers create these cells by depositing one or more extremely thin layers of photovoltaic material onto a foundation material called a substrate. The substrate may be plastic, metal, or glass. The photovoltaic material may be any one of several flexible semiconductors. A layer of photovoltaic material may be a few nanometers to a few microns thick. There are 10,000 microns in a centimeter. The total thickness of a thin-film solar cell is approximately 1 to 10 microns.[2]

Thin-film solar cells have two key advantages over traditional solar cells. Thin-film cells are cheaper to produce, and they are easier to use.

The most common type of traditional solar module is the flat-plate solar panel. It consists of a frame (usually aluminum), a backing and protective capsule (usually a type of plastic), a set of linked solar cells, and a front surface (usually safety glass). Flat-plate solar panels must be mounted onto a structure. They are relatively heavy, fragile, and bulky. Thin-film solar modules, by contrast, are flexible, lightweight, and easy to use in a variety of inconspicuous ways. Manufacturers can build them into construction materials, such as roofing, siding, or awnings. They can even apply semi-transparent thin-film solar modules to windows and skylights. Solar windows look like tinted glass.

It takes much less raw semiconductor material to make thin-film solar cells than to make traditional ones, which are hundreds of times thicker. That makes thin-film cells inherently cheaper.

In addition, thin-film solar cells are simpler to manufacture than traditional solar cells. To create a solar module with traditional cells, manufacturers must first make the cells and then connect the cells individually. The bigger the module, the more cells must be connected. A thin-film solar module, by contrast, is manufactured as a single unit, using a simpler, lower-temperature process. It's no harder to make a 3-by-3-foot (1-by-1 m) thin-film module than it is to make a 2-by-2-inch (5-by-5 cm) module. Manufacturers can easily automate the process to make large quantities.

The main disadvantage of thin-film photovoltaic technology is low efficiency. Currently available thin-film products are 6 to 11 percent efficient.[3] This is approximately half as efficient as traditional solar cells. Researchers can address this limitation by stacking two or more photovoltaic materials together. Different materials capture different wavelengths of sunlight, so one layer can catch some of the energy that another layer misses.

Another drawback is the use of heavy metals in some thin-film solar cells. Thin-film solar cells typically use one of four semiconductor materials. Among these is cadmium telluride. Cadmium is a heavy metal. Heavy metals are poisonous. If they leak into the water or soil, they can damage the environment and cause health problems in humans. Manufacturers must tightly control the production process to make sure they recycle all leftover traces of heavy metals.

Thin-film solar technology developed slowly at first, but it has picked up speed during the past decade. Scientists began developing thin-film solar cells in the 1970s. They have been available in commercial products since the 1990s. In 2005, thin-film products made up only 5 percent of photovoltaic products sold. But the thin-film sector has grown quickly since then. It rose to 25 percent of the photovoltaic market by 2010.[4] Analysts expect that by 2020, thin-film solar cells will have an even larger share of the photovoltaic market.[5] Thin-film products' greatest contribution to the energy industry will likely be bringing down the cost of solar electricity. Lower prices can help photovoltaics compete with electricity generated cheaply by burning fossil fuels.

> **THIN-FILM SEMICONDUCTORS**
>
> The four semiconductors most commonly used in thin-film solar technology are:
>
> 1. Amorphous silicon: This is a non-crystallized form of silicon.
> 2. Copper indium gallium (di)selenide (CIGS): This is a solid solution of the elements copper, indium, gallium, and selenium.
> 3. Cadmium telluride (CdTe): This is a compound made of cadmium and tellurium.
> 4. Organic thin films: These are made from materials that contain carbon.

TRADITIONAL SOLAR

A traditional solar panel made with a glass cover, monocrystalline silicon semiconductor, and a metal backing may be up to 2 inches (5.1 cm) thick.

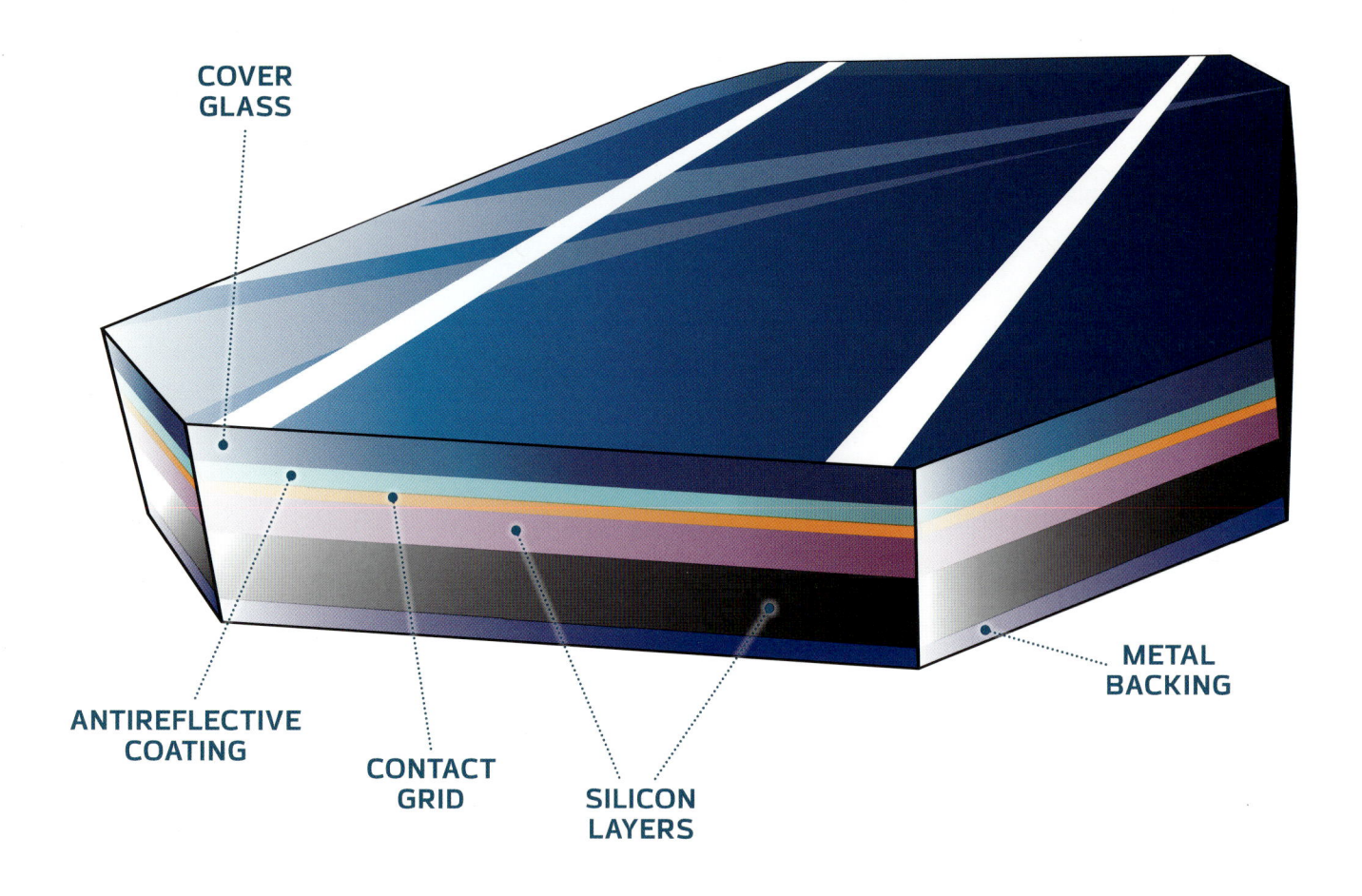

COVER GLASS

METAL BACKING

ANTIREFLECTIVE COATING

CONTACT GRID

SILICON LAYERS

THIN-FILM SOLAR

A thin-film solar panel made with CIGS on foil is wafer-thin—about the thickness of a piece of ordinary aluminum foil.

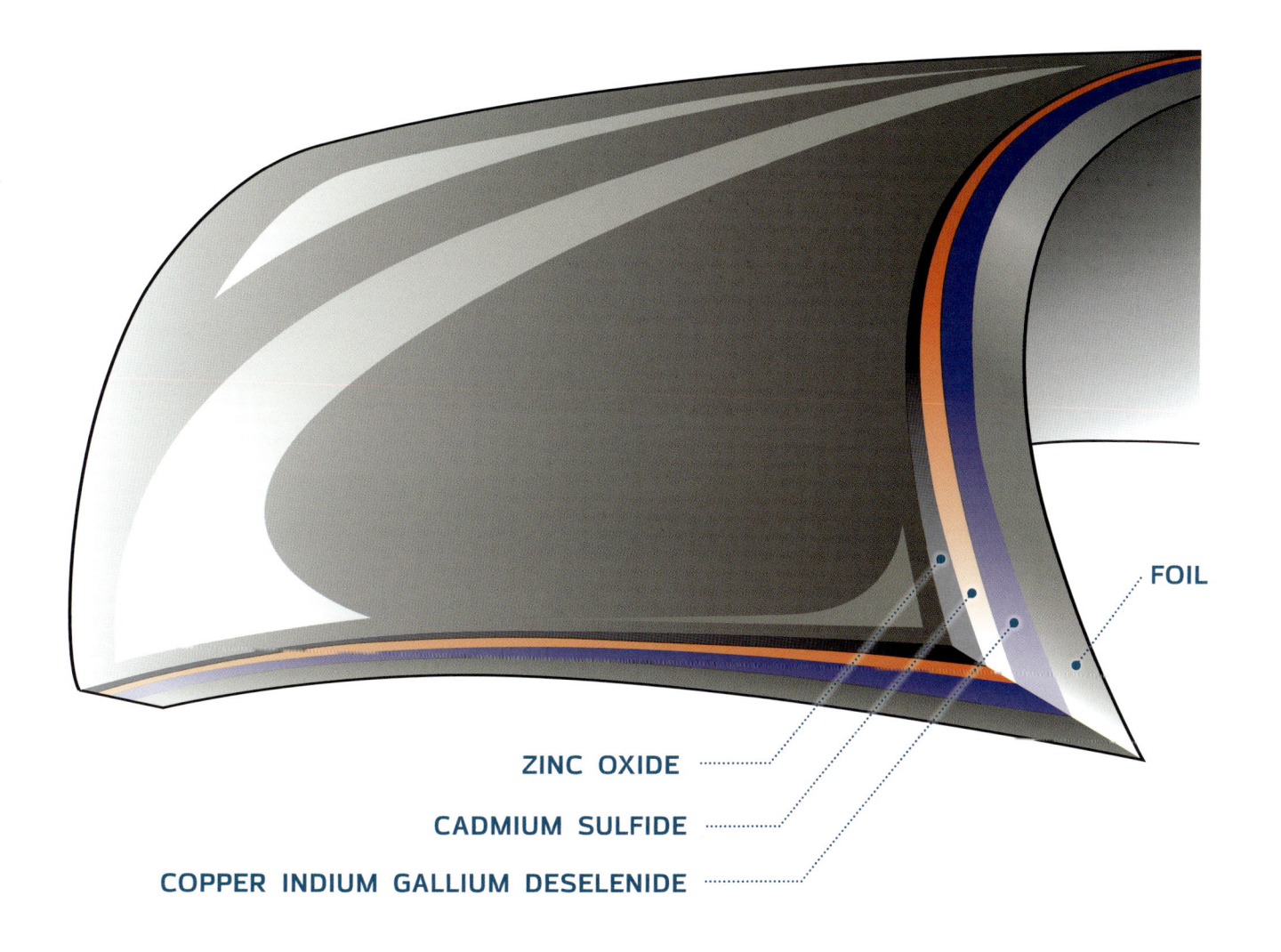

FOIL

ZINC OXIDE

CADMIUM SULFIDE

COPPER INDIUM GALLIUM DESELENIDE

QUANTUM DOTS

A nanotechnology called quantum dots may one day help solar cells make a big leap in usage. However, today it is still in early research stages. Quantum dots are nanoscale blobs of one kind of semiconductor attached to the surface of another kind of semiconductor. They are also called semiconducting nanocrystals. These teensy blobs are important because they can greatly improve the efficiency of a solar cell.

Solar cells have limited efficiency because sunlight consists of a broad range of energy levels. Sunlight is made of photons, or bundles of energy. Some photons are higher energy, and some are lower energy. Solar cells generally harness the energy in the middle of the range. High-level energy that the solar cell can't absorb frees high-energy electrons, or hot electrons, which the solar cell can't hold onto. Hot electrons get lost as heat.

Quantum dots help solar cells harness the energy of hot electrons before that energy escapes the solar cell. Semiconducting nanocrystals, because of their size and shape, behave differently than ordinary semiconductors. Quantum dots can trap hot electrons. And nanocrystals of titanium dioxide, a metal that attracts electrons, can coax hot electrons out of the quantum dots. When quantum dots and titanium dioxide nanocrystals are arranged

Mixed with a solution and put under a UV light, quantum dots glow in brilliant colors.

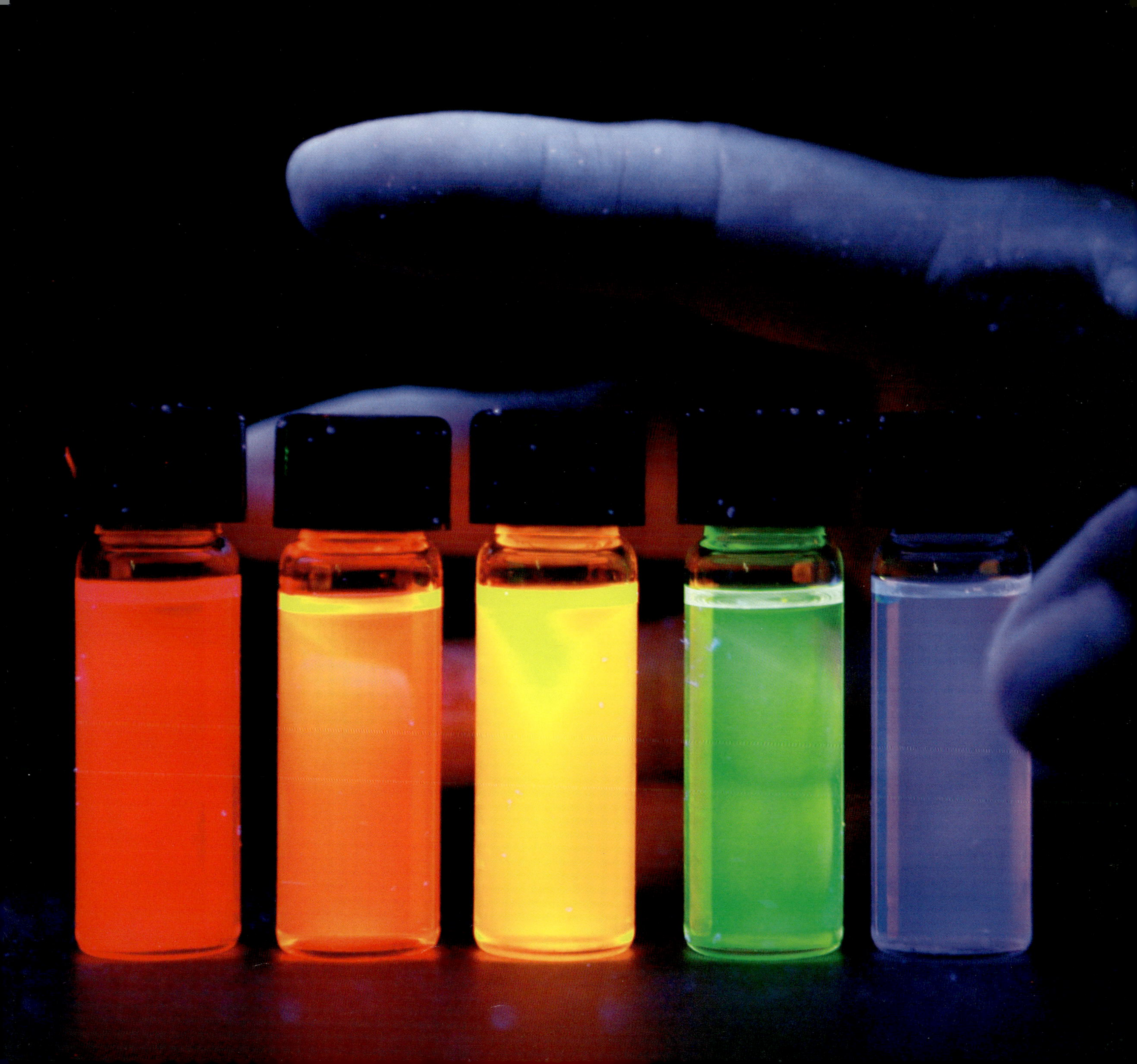

together on the surface of a solar cell, they can create an electric current, or a flow of electrons, from hot electrons.

Using quantum-dot technology, engineers theoretically could develop solar cells that are up to 66 percent efficient.[6] But this technology is still in early research stages. One big hurdle is figuring out how to transfer hot electrons to a conducting wire. According to Xiaoyang Zhu, a chemistry professor at the University of Texas at Austin, "This is science that has really striking implications, but implication is not application yet. I'll be extremely happy if, in my lifetime, I see [hot-carrier cells] on roofs."[7]

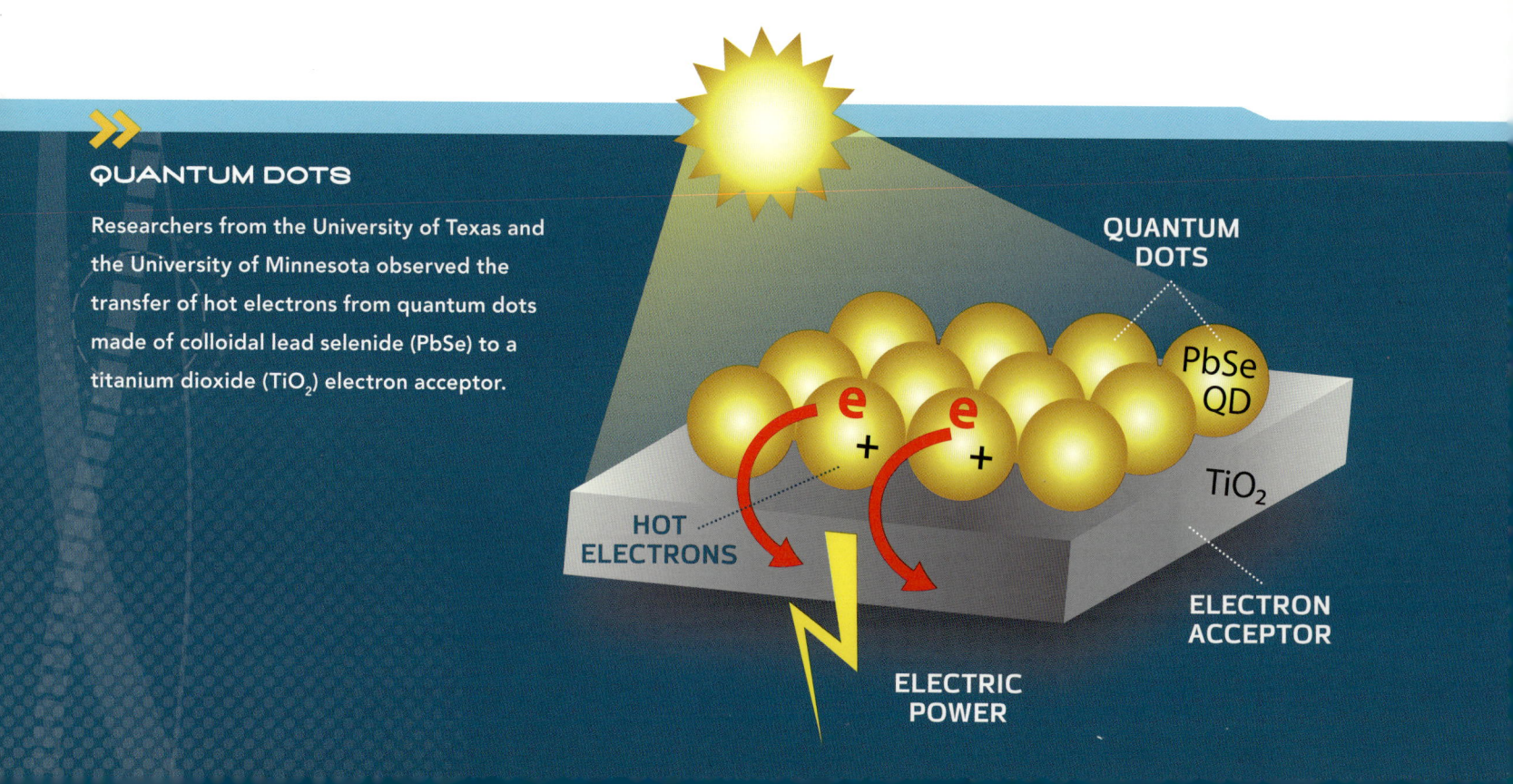

QUANTUM DOTS

Researchers from the University of Texas and the University of Minnesota observed the transfer of hot electrons from quantum dots made of colloidal lead selenide (PbSe) to a titanium dioxide (TiO_2) electron acceptor.

»
Nanosolar's CEO shows components of one of his company's solar panels.

PHOTOVOLTAIC PRINTING

One of the most amazing recent developments in photovoltaics is the printing of solar cells. The company Nanosolar was founded in 2002. By 2007, Nanosolar was producing solar cells with printing press–style machines. These machines print a layer of nanoparticle "ink" made of the semiconductor copper indium gallium diselenide (CIGS) onto metal sheets as thin as aluminum foil. Because the sheets are so thin, Nanosolar can make the panels for approximately 10 percent of the cost of traditional solar panels—and at a rate of several hundred feet per minute.[8]

Scientists at the Massachusetts Institute of Technology (MIT) have demonstrated that they can produce solar modules by printing solar cells on paper. The process uses a printing press to deposit photovoltaic nanoparticle ink on paper.

According to the researchers, a paper solar module consists of 90 percent paper and 10 percent other materials: glue, zinc foil, zinc oxide, carbon, and silicon ink. It is "free from any harmful materials and can be recycled together with aluminum-coated food packages by the existing recycling systems."[9] It can be connected to a device via a simple wire and clip.

"Any fuel engine mostly creates heat and thus wastes the majority of the available energy. . . . I for one have vowed that the Prius I bought six years ago will have been the last fuel-powered car I'd buy in my life. Presently, it is baking in the sun all day while I'm at work. My future all-electric car would charge up while idling under a solar carport."[10]—**Martin Roscheisen, CEO of Nanosolar**

But what's the point of printing solar cells on paper? Who would use them? How efficient are they? And how can paper solar modules possibly stand up to actual use in the real world?

The point, say researchers, is eventually to make the process of manufacturing solar modules so cheap, so easy, and so safe that it can be done nearly anywhere, by nearly anyone, for mere pennies. Paper-printed solar cells do not require ultra-specialized conditions, super-high-tech machinery, or a great deal of skill. Paper solar cells are only approximately 1 percent efficient.[11] That's not a very impressive figure—but it's balanced by the cells' rock-bottom cost and simple production. This electricity could be used to run a vast array of low-power devices. Solar cells could be printed not only on paper, but also on cloth, and made into such ordinary household items as window shades or wallpaper.

The MIT researchers demonstrated that paper solar modules can take a beating. They folded and unfolded one 1,000 times, with no damage to its performance. The solar cells worked even when the module was folded into a paper airplane. And outdoor use is possible as well. Coating the paper with common lamination materials, such as plastic films, can protect the solar modules from the elements.

Paper solar technology, like quantum-dot solar technology, is still in the development stage. The MIT team believes it could be available to consumers within the next few years. Other experts believe the technology will take more time to become viable, if ever.

The company Konarka experimented with printing solar cells on flexible plastic.

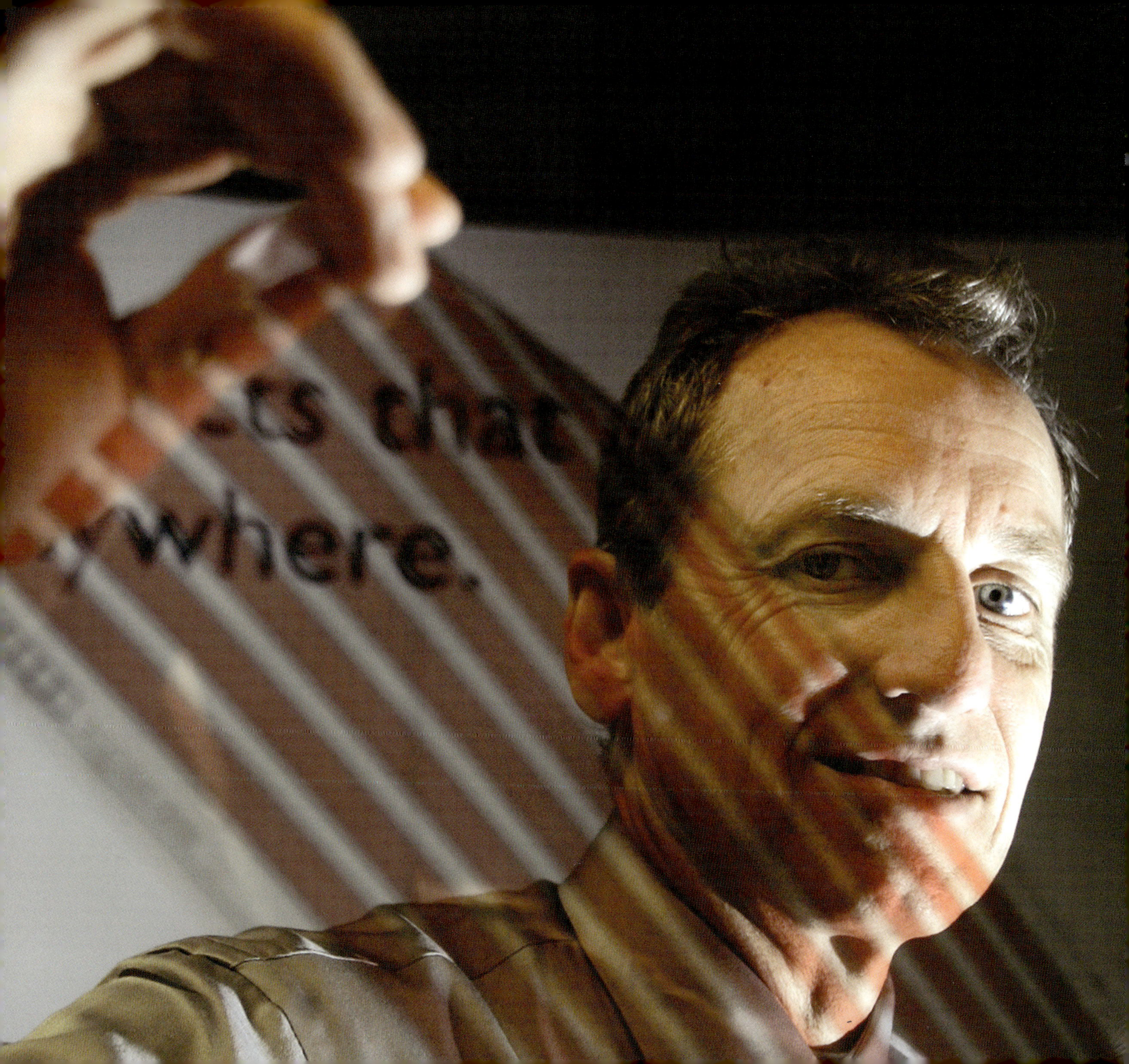
where.

SOLAR IMPULSE

Swiss pilot André Borschberg is soaring thousands of feet over the Alps. It's July 3, 2011, and he's wrapping up a 12-hour flight from Paris, France, to Payerne, Switzerland.

Borschberg's craft is no ordinary airplane. It's the Solar Impulse, which flies on solar energy alone. Borschberg and Bertrand Piccard have been working on it since 2003. By 2014, Borschberg and Piccard hope to fly a similar solar airplane around the globe.

The Solar Impulse seems to be all wing. Its wingspan is 208 feet (63.4 meters), the same as a jumbo jet. The huge wingspan provides space for 11,628 solar cells.[12] These cells convert sunlight into electricity to power every device on the plane.

To conserve energy, the Solar Impulse must be as light as possible. It's made of materials that weigh approximately 3 ounces per square yard (93 g/sq m).[13] Its solar cells are contained in a flexible silicon skin only 0.0006 inches (0.015 m) thick.[14] The airplane's batteries are its heaviest part. Together, they weigh 880 pounds (400 kg). As a result, the plane weighs only 3,527 pounds (1,600 kg) total—approximately the weight of a family car.[15]

The Solar Impulse can fly at night and on cloudy days, thanks to its high-capacity lithium-ion batteries. The Solar Impulse successfully completed a 26-hour flight in July 2010, landing with spare energy in its batteries.

The Solar Impulse is a magnificent sight for scientists as it flies through the sky.

But the Solar Impulse is slow. Borschberg could have driven a car from Paris to Payerne in half the time it took him to fly there. It can't carry passengers or cargo. And because it's so light, air turbulence tosses it around.

Why build such a plane? What's the point of such an impractical vehicle? Practicality is not the point, says the Solar Impulse team. They know that solar cells aren't well suited to airplanes, and they don't expect other researchers to follow in their footsteps. Their goal, rather, is to push the limits of solar technology—and inspire people to think and dream about clean energy.

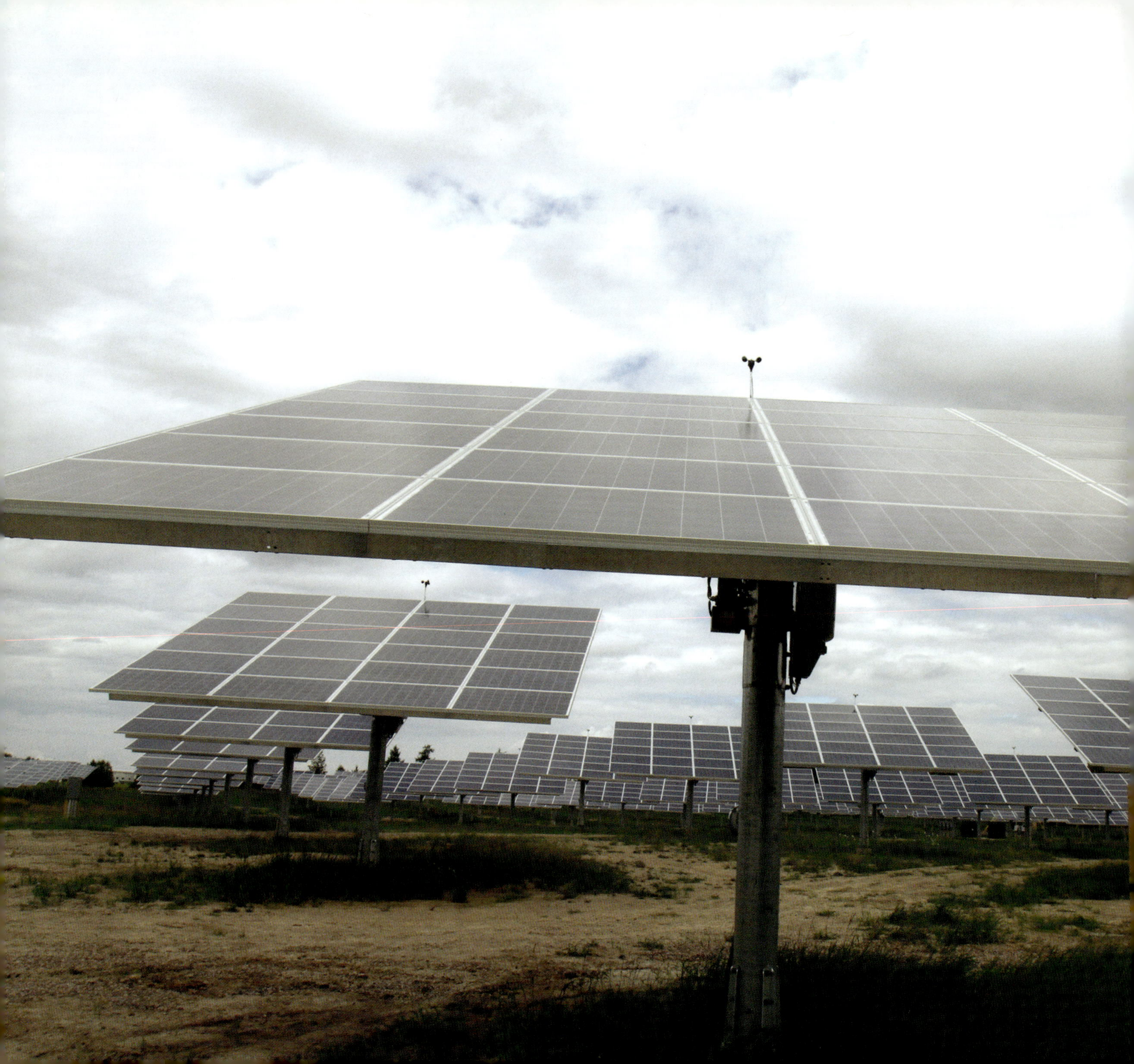

CHAPTER 6

SQUEEZING SUNLIGHT: LUMINESCENT SOLAR CONCENTRATORS

Nanotechnology is just one way to lower the cost and raise the efficiency of a solar module. Another strategy is using a device called a luminescent solar concentrator (LSC). The scientists developing LSC technology are trying to address the following drawbacks of traditional solar cells:

> Solar cells are inherently expensive. Semiconducting materials are costly. Manufacturing the raw materials into solar cells is expensive, too.

> Inefficiency adds expense. Because solar cells are inefficient, it takes a lot of them to generate a usable amount of electricity. The more solar cells a module has, the more expensive it is.

« **Solar trackers help solar panels follow the sunlight, but they are expensive.**

- Sunlight is hard to catch. Traditional solar cells work best when direct sunlight hits them straight on. But sometimes it's cloudy. Clouds scatter sunlight, creating diffuse instead of direct light. And Earth is in constant motion, so the angle of sunlight hitting any surface changes constantly. A fixed, or motionless, solar module, therefore, "misses" a lot of sunlight.

- Tracking the sun is tricky, too. To receive as much direct sunlight as possible, a solar module can use a tracker. A tracker is a device that either moves the module or moves mirrors or lenses that focus sunlight on the module. However, trackers are very expensive. They need to follow the sun perfectly—a tall order—in order to work properly. They also tend to overheat solar cells. This makes expensive cooling systems necessary.

The goal of an LSC is to lower the cost of solar power in two ways. An LSC uses fewer solar cells, and it maximizes the amount of sunlight each cell converts into electricity. An LSC does this by absorbing a wider range of solar energy and concentrating—or squeezing—that energy before feeding it to solar cells.

"If [solar trackers] are a few tenths of a degree off from perfection, the power output of the system drops drastically."[1]—**Penn State University electrical engineering professor Chris Giebink, 2011**

HOW AN LSC WORKS

An LSC is a broad, flat device, like a flat-plate solar panel. But that's where the resemblance ends. An LSC is made of different materials arranged in a different way. It has three main parts: a sheet of glass, fluorescent dye, and solar cells. A thin film of dye coats the glass. The solar cells lie along the edge of the glass.

LSCs work because of luminescence. Luminescence is the ability to emit light without heat. Many different things, such as chemical reactions, can cause luminescence. As a result, there are many different forms of luminescence.

Fluorescence is one form. When light hits a fluorescent substance, the substance absorbs the light and then reemits most of that energy as light of a different wavelength. For example,

COMMON FLUORESCENT SUBSTANCES

Many ordinary objects and materials fluoresce under ultraviolet light. Here are a few:

- antifreeze
- blood
- chlorophyll in plants
- dark spots on ripe bananas
- petroleum jelly
- some laundry detergents and household cleaners
- teeth whiteners
- tonic water
- US $20 bill
- urine
- vitamin A and all the B vitamins
- white paper

> **Counterfeit money is often tested under ultraviolet light.**

white paper is usually treated with fluorescent compounds to make it look whiter and brighter. If you place it under a black light, the fluorescent materials in the paper will absorb the ultraviolet light, which has a short wavelength and is invisible to the human eye. Then they will emit light of a longer wavelength, which is visible to the human eye as fluorescence.

When sunlight hits the LSC, the dye absorbs it. Because the dye is a fluorescent substance, it converts most of the solar energy into a different wavelength and reemits it. The emitted light doesn't radiate back out into the air, though; it stays within the film of dye. But the dye doesn't reabsorb the light; instead, the dye moves that emitted light toward the edge of the glass.

The dye uses two techniques to accomplish this. The dye film's thickness changes microscopically across the sheet. The pattern resembles a repeating staircase. When the dye emits light, the light bounces away from the location where it was emitted. The dye film contains a molecule with aluminum in it. The aluminum in the molecules causes the dye to emit light waves at a frequency the dye can't reabsorb.

In this way, the dye acts as a waveguide. A waveguide is a device that captures radiation and moves the waves of energy along a specific path to a specific destination.

Eventually the light waves reach the edge of the glass. There they enter the solar cells. The solar cells convert the light waves into electricity.

PROS AND CONS

LSCs have several advantages over traditional photovoltaic modules. An LSC can collect not only direct sunlight, but also diffuse sunlight. That means it will work on a sunny day, a cloudy day, or any kind of in-between day.

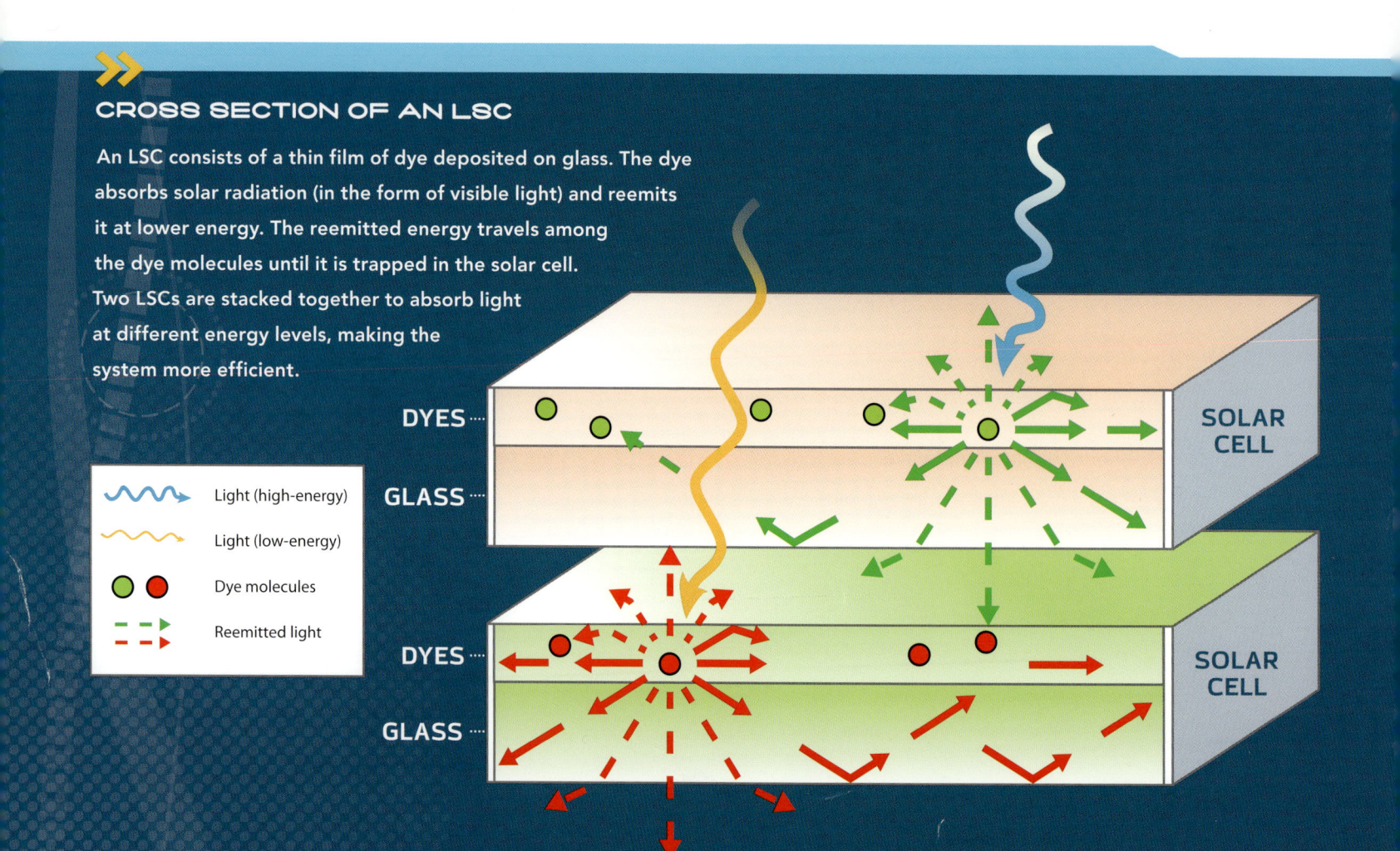

CROSS SECTION OF AN LSC

An LSC consists of a thin film of dye deposited on glass. The dye absorbs solar radiation (in the form of visible light) and reemits it at lower energy. The reemitted energy travels among the dye molecules until it is trapped in the solar cell. Two LSCs are stacked together to absorb light at different energy levels, making the system more efficient.

- Light (high-energy)
- Light (low-energy)
- Dye molecules
- Reemitted light

DYES
GLASS
SOLAR CELL
DYES
GLASS
SOLAR CELL

An LSC collects more sunlight per solar cell than a traditional solar module. A solar cell at the edge of the LSC absorbs ten times more light than a cell of the same size without an LSC. Each solar cell receives much more sunlight, which means an LSC needs fewer cells. Fewer cells means lower cost.

Because LSCs are made mainly of glass and do not require solar trackers, they can be integrated into construction materials. They could be used as windows or siding, or on other vertical spaces in cities, enabling large amounts of currently unused space to generate electricity.

However, LSC technology is not ready for widespread use. LSCs break very quickly. Laboratory models have lasted only about three months. That's not nearly long enough for consumers, who expect solar modules to last for years or even decades.

Also, researchers working on LSC technology do not believe that they've hit on the ideal thickness pattern for the LSC's dye film. The repeating-staircase pattern works, but scientists think a more complicated approach would work even better. In the meantime, silicon cells are becoming ever cheaper, meaning this new technology will have to deliver more energy more cheaply for it to become commercially viable.

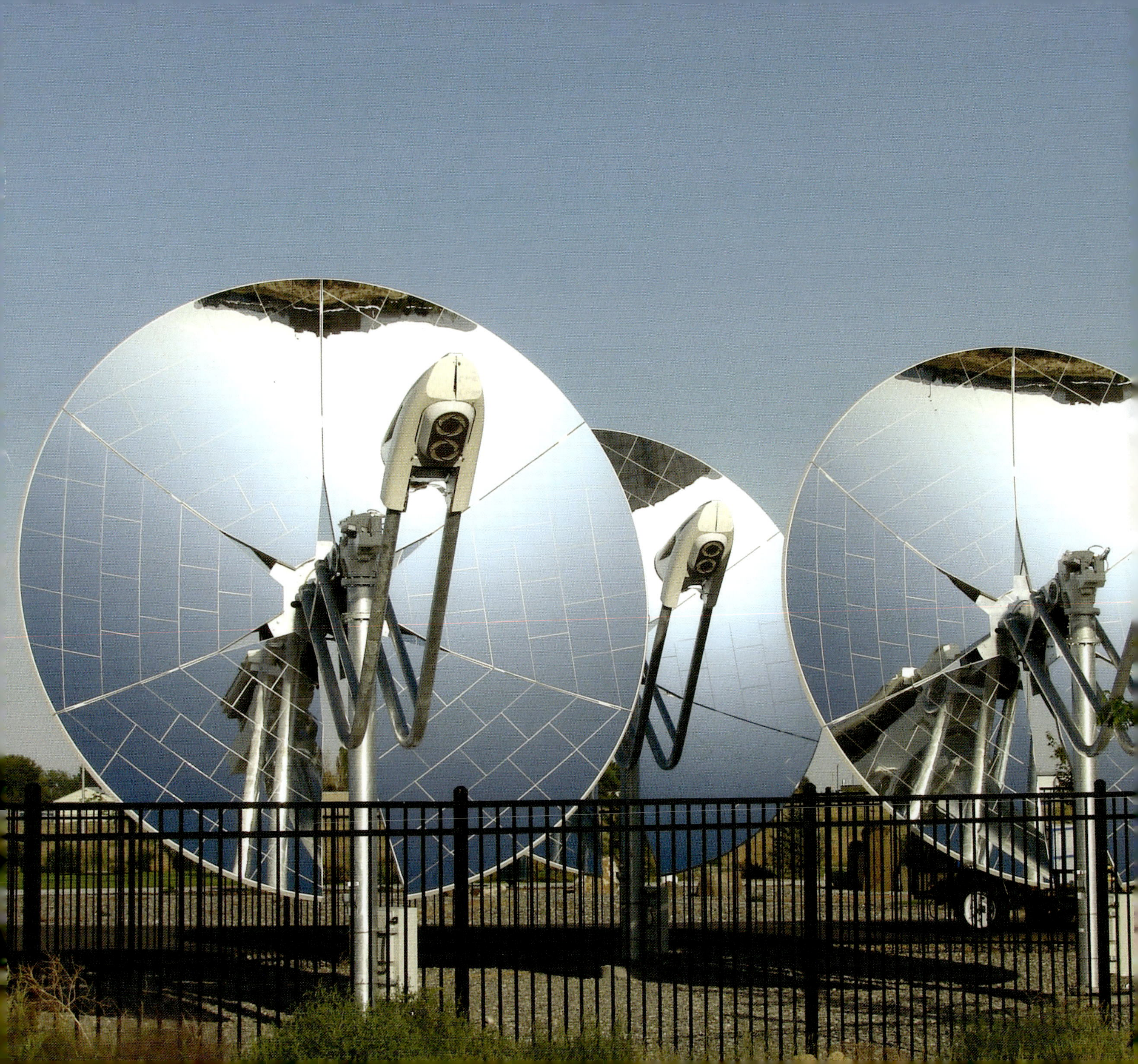

CHAPTER 7

HEATING THINGS UP: SOLAR THERMAL INNOVATIONS

In the early twenty-first century, photovoltaic innovations have dominated solar energy news. It's no surprise. The general public is more familiar with photovoltaic energy. Most Americans, for example, have seen solar panels on buildings but not solar thermal devices. And photovoltaic innovations are indeed impressive. The capabilities of extremely small nanostructures and nanoparticles boggle the human mind. But a lot of innovation is happening in solar thermal technology too. Scientists are taking a variety of approaches to improve the performance of solar thermal devices and to make solar thermal a more versatile source of power.

TYPES OF SOLAR THERMAL POWER PLANTS

In order to provide large amounts of heat, sunlight must be concentrated. Solar thermal power plants concentrate sunlight in three main ways: a linear system, a dish-engine

« **Solar thermal power plants collect sunlight to convert it into electricity.**

system, and a power tower system. Solar thermal plants then use the heat to start a process that powers a turbine to produce electricity.

- A *linear system* concentrates sunlight with long rectangular mirrors. The mirrors may be either parabolic troughs (U-shaped mirrors) or Fresnel reflectors (shallow troughs or flat mirrors with reflective ridges). The mirrors focus sunlight on tubes that run the length of the mirrors. The focused sunlight heats a fluid in the tubes, which is then used to boil water and run a steam turbine. The steam turbine produces electricity.

- A *dish-engine system* concentrates sunlight with a mirror that resembles a large satellite dish. The dish focuses sunlight onto a receiver, which contains a gas or liquid called the working fluid. The heated working fluid expands and moves pistons inside an engine, which creates mechanical power. The mechanical power then runs a generator to produce electricity.

- A *power tower system* uses a large field of flat, sun-tracking mirrors called heliostats to focus sunlight onto a receiver atop a tower. The focused sunlight heats a fluid in the tubes—usually water or molten salt—which is then used to boil water and run a steam turbine. The steam turbine produces electricity.

This power tower system is located in the Mojave Desert.

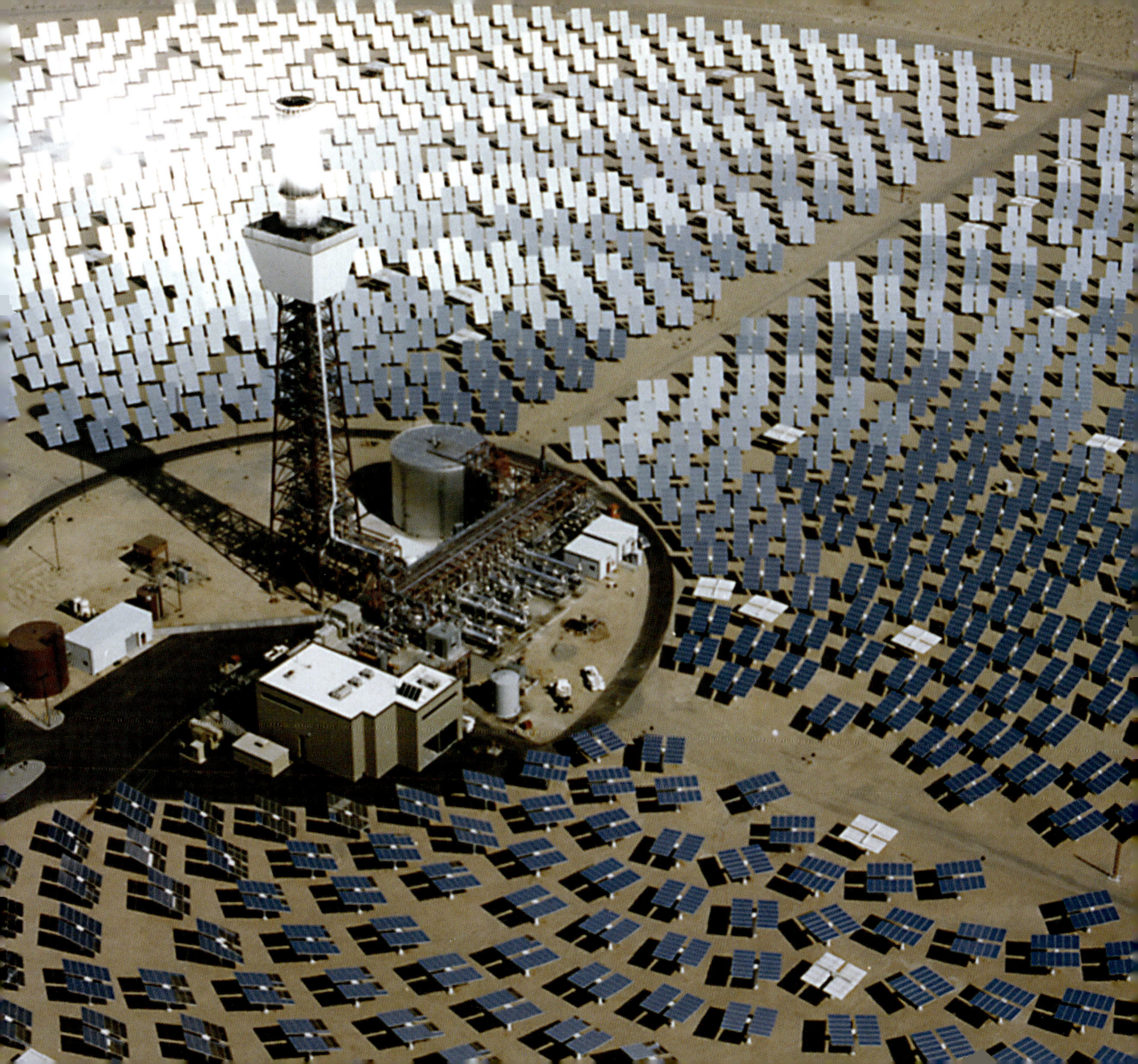

In 2012, approximately 60 solar thermal power plants existed in the world. All of them were large operations, comparable to traditional power plants. The majority were in Spain. Sixteen were in the United States, while others were in Algeria, Australia, Egypt, Morocco, and Thailand. Approximately 30 solar thermal power plants were under construction. The majority were in Spain. Five were in the United States, while others were in China, India, and the United Arab Emirates.[1]

BETTER MIRRORS FOR LINEAR SYSTEMS

Most solar thermal systems in use today—approximately 90 percent—are linear systems. Of the remaining 10 percent, most are power tower systems.[2] Although they work differently, both use a large field of mirrors to focus sunlight.

Traditionally, solar thermal power plants have used glass mirrors mounted on metal structures. But glass isn't perfect. According to Gary Jorgenson, a senior scientist at the National Renewable Energy Laboratory, "Glass is highly durable, but is heavy and hard to shape without added cost."[3]

The reflective layer in a glass mirror is usually aluminum or silver. Silver is preferable, because it is the most reflective of all metals within the right light wavelengths. But silver is a relatively soft metal. It scratches easily. And over time, silver is also susceptible to damage from

Reflectors at SEGS VI are testing a new reflective film.

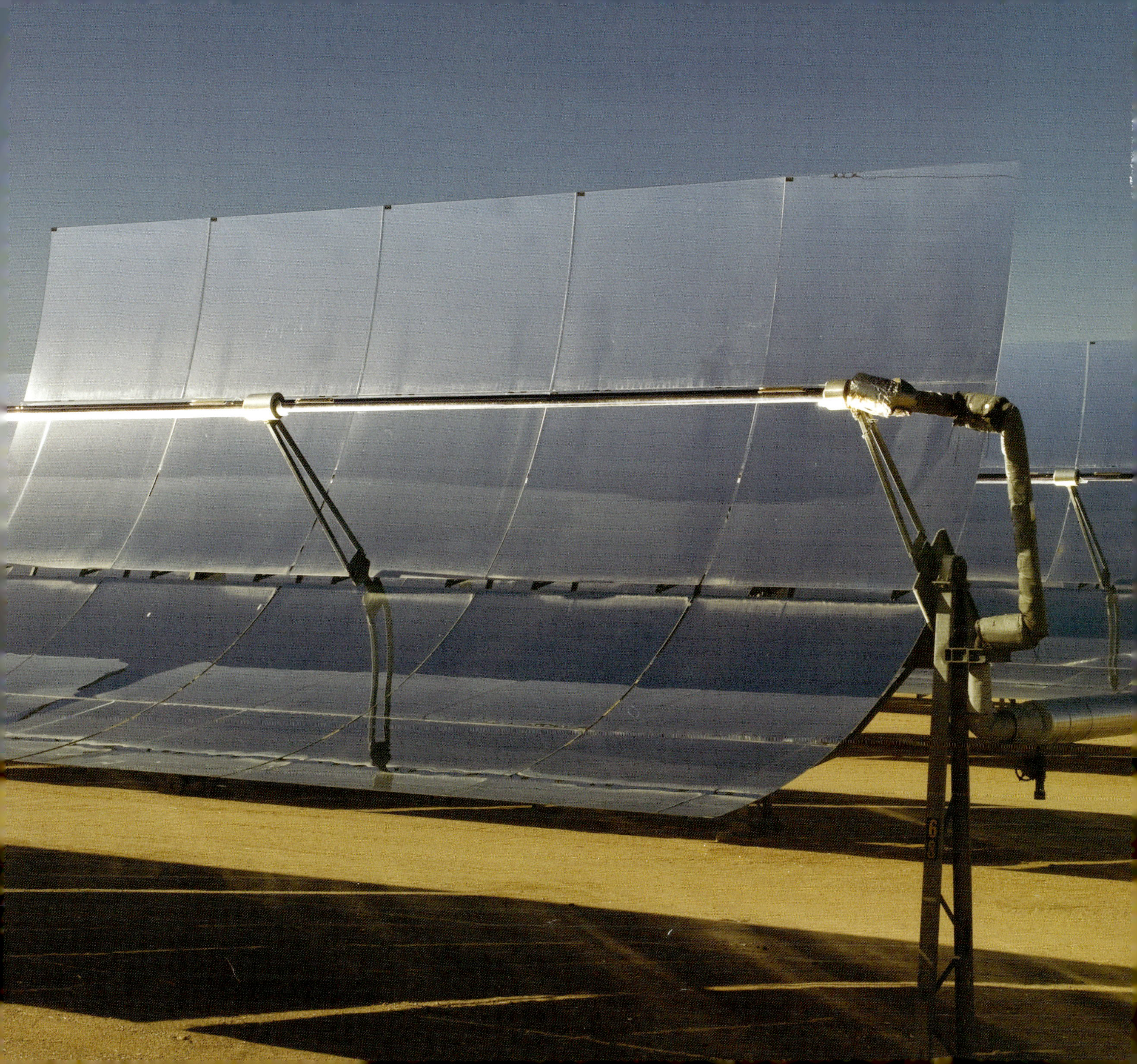
68

ultraviolet radiation, tarnishing, and other types of corrosion from ordinary substances in Earth's atmosphere, such as oxygen, chlorine, sulfur, ozone, and humidity. When a silvered mirror becomes scratched, tarnished, or corroded, its reflectivity deteriorates.

So in the late 1990s, NREL's Jorgenson and Randy Gee, chief technology officer at a company called SkyFuel, began trying to build a better reflector. They used NREL's facilities to test hundreds of possible materials that might offer low weight, low cost, durability, and flexibility. A few years later, they had all the data they needed.

The researchers settled on a thin film made of a silver layer within multiple layers of plastic films that protect the silver from weather, pollution, and ultraviolet damage. The film has an adhesive backing so it can be applied to smooth surfaces, such as aluminum sheets.

Gee explained that the mirror film "has the same performance as the heavy glass mirrors, but at a much lower cost and much lower weight. It also is much easier to deploy and install."[4] The cost of reflectors made with this film is approximately 30 percent lower than that of traditional glass reflectors.[5]

The film became available for others to buy in 2009. And so far, it seems to be delivering on its promise of durability and high reflectivity. Testing demonstrates that it reflects 93 percent of the sunlight that hits it.[6] Accelerated weathering simulations show that it should last at least 30 years. The film is also undergoing a real-world trial on the parabolic trough reflectors at SEGS VI, a solar thermal power plant in California's Mojave Desert. Installed in late 2002, the film showed no significant corrosion, deterioration, or loss of reflectivity when tested in 2010.

GRAPHITE: NOT JUST FOR PENCILS ANYMORE

Linear solar thermal systems and power tower systems both use liquid as a heat transfer fluid. The heat transfer fluid is usually water or thermal oil (a type of synthetic, or artificial, oil).

Ideally, the heat transfer fluid is a good sunlight absorber. Different substances absorb sunlight at different rates. Generally speaking, dark-colored substances and objects absorb sunlight better than light-colored substances and objects do.

COLOR AND SUNLIGHT

When sunlight hits a surface, the object may reflect the light, absorb it, or transmit it (let it pass through)—or a combination of these. Various surfaces look different to the human eye because of differences in the way they absorb and reflect sunlight.

Most objects are not luminous; that is, they don't produce light on their own. So in order to see these objects, we need light from some other source to hit them. The color of a nonluminous object depends on which wavelengths of visible light it absorbs and which wavelengths it reflects. Our eyes see the reflected wavelengths.

Fresh snow, for example, looks white because it reflects all the wavelengths of visible light, which combine to make white light. A green leaf looks green because it reflects the green wavelength of visible light and absorbs the other wavelengths. A black rock looks black because it absorbs all the wavelengths of visible light.

> ### GRAPHITE
>
> Graphite is actually a very high-grade coal. People don't usually use it as a fuel, though, because it's hard to ignite. We use graphite mainly as pencil lead, in solid form, and as a lubricant, in powdered form.

At Arizona State University (ASU), a group of engineers is trying to boost the efficiency of solar thermal systems by helping them capture more heat from sunlight. First the researchers made a significant change from traditional solar thermal systems. Usually the heat transfer fluid flows through a black tube. The ASU researchers instead used a transparent tube. Then, the researchers added nanoparticles of graphite to thermal oil. Graphite is a naturally occurring mineral. It is a form of carbon, as coal is. So sunlight heats the fluid directly instead of heating a black tube, which then heats the fluid.

The researchers chose to add graphite for two key reasons. It's black, so it's very good at absorbing sunlight. Thermal oils are already good heat absorbers; adding graphite improves their absorption ability. Graphite is also a common material. Because it's common, it's cheap—approximately one dollar per gram. And not much is needed. To improve heat absorption, an effective mixture includes approximately 99 percent oil, 1 percent surfactant (a substance similar to powdered laundry soap), and 0.001 to 0.1 percent graphite nanoparticles.[7]

In laboratory tests, the ASU team found that the graphite nanoparticles did, in fact, help thermal oil absorb more light. The graphite increased heat absorption by 5 to 10 percent.[8] "We estimate that this could mean up to $3.5 million per year more revenue for a 100-megawatt solar power plant," said researcher Robert Taylor.[9]

Scientists hope using graphite successfully will serve as a springboard to using coal soot. Coal soot is composed of tiny carbon particles left over from burning coal. It is similar to graphite powder. "It might also be possible to filter out nanoparticles of soot, which have similar absorbing potential, from coal power plants for use in solar [thermal] systems," explained Taylor. He went on, "I think that idea is particularly attractive: using a pollutant to harvest clean, green solar energy."[10]

The benefits of adding graphite or soot nanoparticles to solar thermal heat transfer fluids include low cost, improved heat absorption—thus better efficiency—and the possibility of recycling pollutants. According to Taylor, the

> **WHAT'S A WATT?**
>
> People measure the production and use of electricity in watts. A watt is a unit whose name honors James Watt, the inventor who perfected the steam engine in the eighteenth century. A laptop computer needs approximately 50 watts. A microwave oven needs approximately 750 to 1,100 watts. A hair dryer needs approximately 1,200 to 1,875 watts. A kilowatt is 1,000 watts. A megawatt is 1 million watts. A gigawatt is 1 billion watts.[11]

main drawback to his team's idea is that it wouldn't be cost effective for linear solar thermal systems. The cost of replacing many, many receiver tubes of heat transfer fluid would outweigh the potential savings. The concept works best for a power tower system, which has just one large receiver. As of 2011, the ASU team was unable to predict when the technology might be available commercially.

PLEASE PASS THE SALT

In addition to being a good heat absorber, a heat transfer fluid should also have a low viscosity—it should flow easily—and it should have high thermal capacity—it should be able to hold a lot of heat.

Both water and thermal oil have low viscosity and high thermal capacity. But neither can receive or store large amounts of energy, because both have a relatively narrow temperature range at which they remain liquid. Once they become gaseous, they release their stored energy. Solar thermal power systems can reach very high temperatures—hot enough that water becomes a gas and oils start to break down. If a solar thermal plant's heat transfer fluid is water or oil, it can't absorb as much sunlight as possible. In other words, it's forced to run inefficiently.

To address this problem, scientists have turned their attention to molten salts. Salts make up a special category of minerals. This category includes not only table salt but also several

Solar Millennium is on the cutting edge of molten salt technology.

other salts. Most salts melt only at high temperatures. For example, table salt melts into liquid at approximately 1,472 degrees Fahrenheit (800°C) and doesn't turn into vapor until it gets a lot hotter than that. Because salts stay in liquid form at very high temperatures, they can receive and store a great deal of sunlight. Put simply: they can take as much energy as the sun dishes out.

This technology is already in use commercially. For example, the German company Solar Millennium developed a power plant called Andasol 1 near Granada, Spain. This plant uses linear concentrators with thermal oil in their receiver tubes, then transfers the heat from the oil to molten salt for storage. Andasol 1's salt is a mixture of sodium and potassium nitrate.

It can store enough heat to keep the 50-megawatt power plant generating electricity at full capacity for nearly eight hours after sunset. Sven Moormann, a spokesman for Solar Millennium, explained, "The hours of production are nearly double [those of a solar-thermal] power plant without storage."[12]

> "Although solar cells cannot generate electricity at night, people don't need as much electricity at night either when they are asleep. It is good that solar cells provide electricity during the time of day when people need it the most."[13]—**Mike McGehee, professor at Stanford University Center for Advanced Molecular Photovoltaics**

The ability to store solar energy and keep producing electricity through the night is a major breakthrough for solar power. Ever since people began using sunlight to produce electricity, we have struggled with the challenge of solar energy storage. The sun is a dependable source of power in places that receive lots of strong, consistent sunlight. But places with cloudy climates and places far from Earth's equator get much less sunlight. And regardless of location, solar devices receive no sunlight after sunset. For solar power to work all over the world and around the clock, we need to be able to store large amounts of energy. Batteries are impractical because they need to be very large to store the quantity of energy harnessed by a solar power plant. What is more: many types of batteries release energy too slowly to be useful in a power plant, which needs to generate a lot of steady electricity all day and night. In addition, chemical batteries contain toxic substances, are expensive to manufacture, and don't last long.

In addition to their energy-storage ability, molten salts have two other key advantages. Most of them are common, cheap, and widely available. For example, farmers are quite familiar with the combination of sodium and potassium nitrate used at Andasol 1. Farmers use this compound in its solid form as a fertilizer to help their plants grow. And salts overall are relatively safe for the environment compared to other chemicals. While a major salt leak would create a mess, it would not cause a toxic disaster.

Molten salt heat transfer fluids do have their drawbacks, though. Their biggest disadvantage is their high melting point. Salts are useful as heat transfer fluids only when they're melted into liquid form. If solid salt melts at 284 degrees Fahrenheit (140°C), that means the same salt in liquid form freezes, or solidifies, when it drops below that temperature. There's no place on Earth's surface that has a climate hot enough to keep salt in its liquid state. So a solar thermal power plant using molten salt must have some way to keep the salt hot enough to prevent freezing.

This isn't difficult in a power tower system. Because of its centralized design, a power tower system can maintain very high temperatures—up to 1,000 degrees Fahrenheit (535°C)—and use molten salts directly as a heat transfer fluid.[14]

But it's not practical to use most salts in the receiver tubes of linear systems. There's so much length of tube in a linear system that it's tricky and expensive to design the tubes in a way that keeps the salt hot enough. So at present, most linear systems use oil in the receiver tubes and molten salt for storage only, as the Andasol 1 power plant does. However, linear systems that use oil as a heat transfer fluid and molten salt for heat storage are inherently inefficient. Thermal oil can heat only to approximately 752 degrees Fahrenheit (400°C), but molten salt can take a lot more heat than that.[15] The salt doesn't get used to its full potential.

Scientists are working hard to develop salts that melt at lower temperatures. A lower melting point reduces the risk of freezing—especially on cold nights—and thus reduces the need for complex, expensive precautions. Such salts can

SOLAR PONDS

The solar pond is another type of solar thermal system that takes advantage of salt's high thermal capacity. Solar ponds must be very salty. When they absorb sunlight, the heat collects at the bottom of the pond where the water is densest and saltiest. Solar ponds are very efficient at storing the sun's heat. People can tap into this hot water for heating or generating electricity.

be used more easily as heat transfer fluids in linear systems, boosting the systems' efficiency even more.

In Italy, the company Archimede is developing three power plants that will use such innovative salts in linear solar thermal systems. These plants will use a three-salt compound with a melting point of 248 degrees Fahrenheit (120°C).[16] Germany's Solar Millennium is developing a similar salt. And the United States' Sandia National Laboratories has produced small amounts of a new salt compound that melts below 212 degrees Fahrenheit (100°C).[17]

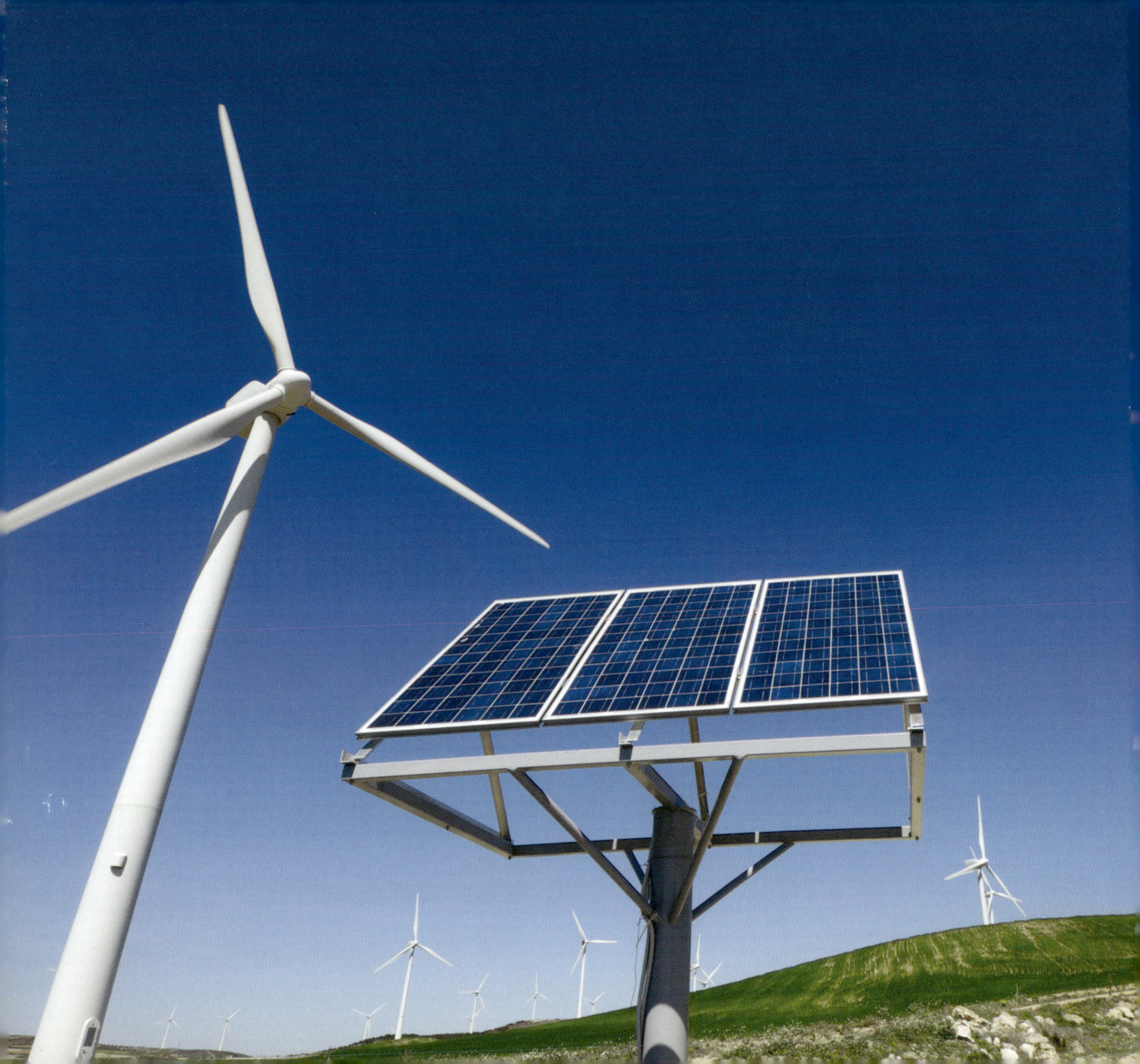

CHAPTER 8

SOLAR POWER TODAY AND TOMORROW

Solar power has been growing quickly in the United States. In 2010, solar power was one of the United States' two fastest-growing electricity generation technologies. (The other was wind power.) That year, US photovoltaic capacity grew 71 percent from the preceding year, while US solar thermal capacity grew 18 percent.[1] Unsurprisingly, most of the United States' solar electricity generation happens in its sunny southwestern states. At present, solar energy produces approximately 0.1 percent of the electricity generated in the United States.[2]

Solar power has been growing fast globally too. Solar power was the world's fastest-growing renewable electricity generation technology in 2010. That year global photovoltaic capacity grew 90 percent from the preceding year, while global solar thermal capacity grew 83 percent. Spain and the United States were top producers

« **Alternative energy is becoming a top priority for many nations.**

TOP SOLAR STATES[6]

RANK	PHOTOVOLTAIC	SOLAR THERMAL
1	California	California
2	New Jersey	Florida
3	Colorado	Nevada
4	Arizona	Arizona
5	Nevada	Colorado

TOP SOLAR NATIONS[7]

RANK	PHOTOVOLTAIC	SOLAR THERMAL
1	Germany	Spain
2	Spain	United States
3	Japan	
4	Italy	
5	United States	

of both kinds of solar electricity.[3] Solar energy currently accounts for approximately 0.5 percent of all the electricity generated in the world.[4]

Growth in solar electricity generation is due in part to aggressive government policies promoting solar energy and growth in solar device manufacturing. Countries with aggressive solar policies, such as Germany, Japan, and Spain, lead the world in installing and using photovoltaic technology. In the same way, US states with strong business incentives for solar power lead the United States in installing and using solar devices. US photovoltaic manufacturers currently have a small share of the world market. China and Taiwan are the market leaders. They produce nearly 60 percent of the world's solar cells.[5]

Chinese workers manufacture photovoltaic cells.

Researchers estimate that by 2025, solar energy could provide 10 percent of the United States' electricity. They predict that 8 percent will come from photovoltaic technology, while 2 percent will come from solar thermal plants.[8] The cost of solar photovoltaic systems is dropping, while the price of electricity generated from fossil fuels is rising. As a result, energy analysts project that solar power and conventional power sources will cost essentially the same in many parts of the United States by 2015.

Global energy analysts project similar growth in world solar power. The International Energy Agency (IEA) estimates that by 2050, solar energy will provide approximately 22 percent of the world's electricity. The IEA predicts that 11 percent will come from distributed solar power, or small solar installations such as those on homes and other buildings. Another 11 percent will come from centralized solar power plants. The agency says that globally, the cost of distributed photovoltaic power could compete with traditional electricity by 2020. It predicts that solar thermal plants could compete with coal and nuclear power plants by 2030.[9]

In order to achieve this growth, governments will need to keep providing incentives for developing and using solar power until the industry is big enough to stand on its own. As the industry gets larger, the costs naturally come down, because companies learn how to make new factories more efficient. The government can help accelerate this process by providing incentives.

Meanwhile, the solar industry must keep trying to improve the efficiency and lower the manufacturing cost of solar devices. Better efficiency and cheaper manufacturing will steadily bring down the cost of solar power for consumers. To increase the consumer appeal of solar power, companies will need to streamline solar installations to make them less obtrusive both visually and spatially. Companies must also simplify the process of buying, installing, operating, and maintaining small solar installations. Costs will come down if solar cells are installed in housing developments when the houses are being built. It is easier to run the wires from the roof before the walls are put up. Also, the company can save money if it installs cells on every house in the neighborhood at the same time instead of traveling to do one installation at a time.

Finally, electric utilities must figure out how to integrate solar power into the "grid." A nation's grid is its power infrastructure, or the combination of networks that carry electricity from power plants to consumers. The grid includes wires, substations, transformers, switches, and much more. How will they link new solar power plants to the existing grid? Should smaller private installations link with the grid so they can share—and profit from—any excess power they generate?

DISTRIBUTED SOLAR SNAPSHOT

PROS:
- Distributed solar loses no electricity through transmission.
- The user owns the system and reaps its economic benefits, both by generating electricity on-site and by selling extra electricity to power companies.
- It is less vulnerable to natural and human-made disasters.
- It makes use of otherwise wasted space, such as rooftops.
- It allows more room for technical innovation.
- A rooftop, canopy, or facade installation shades the space or structure beneath it.
- Small solar is cheaper and easier to install and thus more likely to be installed.

CONS:
- Small solar installations make small amounts of electricity, so it takes a lot of them to generate large amounts of power.
- Distributed solar needs more engineers and workers per megawatt, so its up-front costs are higher.
- It is not a high-profit business.
- It requires government and business to invest in collective power storage devices to make the most of generated electricity.

CENTRALIZED SOLAR SNAPSHOT

PROS:
- Solar power plants produce large amounts of electricity for the grid.
- They need fewer engineers and workers per megawatt, so their up-front costs are lower.
- They can provide income for their owners.
- They can replace fossil fuel power plants, producing similar amounts of energy with less environmental cost.

CONS:
- Solar power plants require large areas of rural land.
- Their construction can be disruptive.
- They require additional construction of substations and power lines.
- Prolonged cloud cover can interfere with electricity generation.
- Some electricity is lost through transmission over long distances.
- Solar power plants may be obtrusive for local residents and may disrupt ecosystems.

Despite these challenges, solar energy has a bright future. Philip Eames, director of the Center for Renewable Energy Systems Technology at Loughborough University in the United Kingdom, is quite optimistic. He observed in an interview with CNN, "I've seen predictions before, and they are becoming more and more bullish as the technology develops." He noted that solar energy costs have plummeted in the past few years. And he predicted that prices will continue to fall, thereby increasing the installation and use of solar energy. He believes "solar power's time is starting to come."[10]

Solar power is becoming more and more popular as a home energy source.

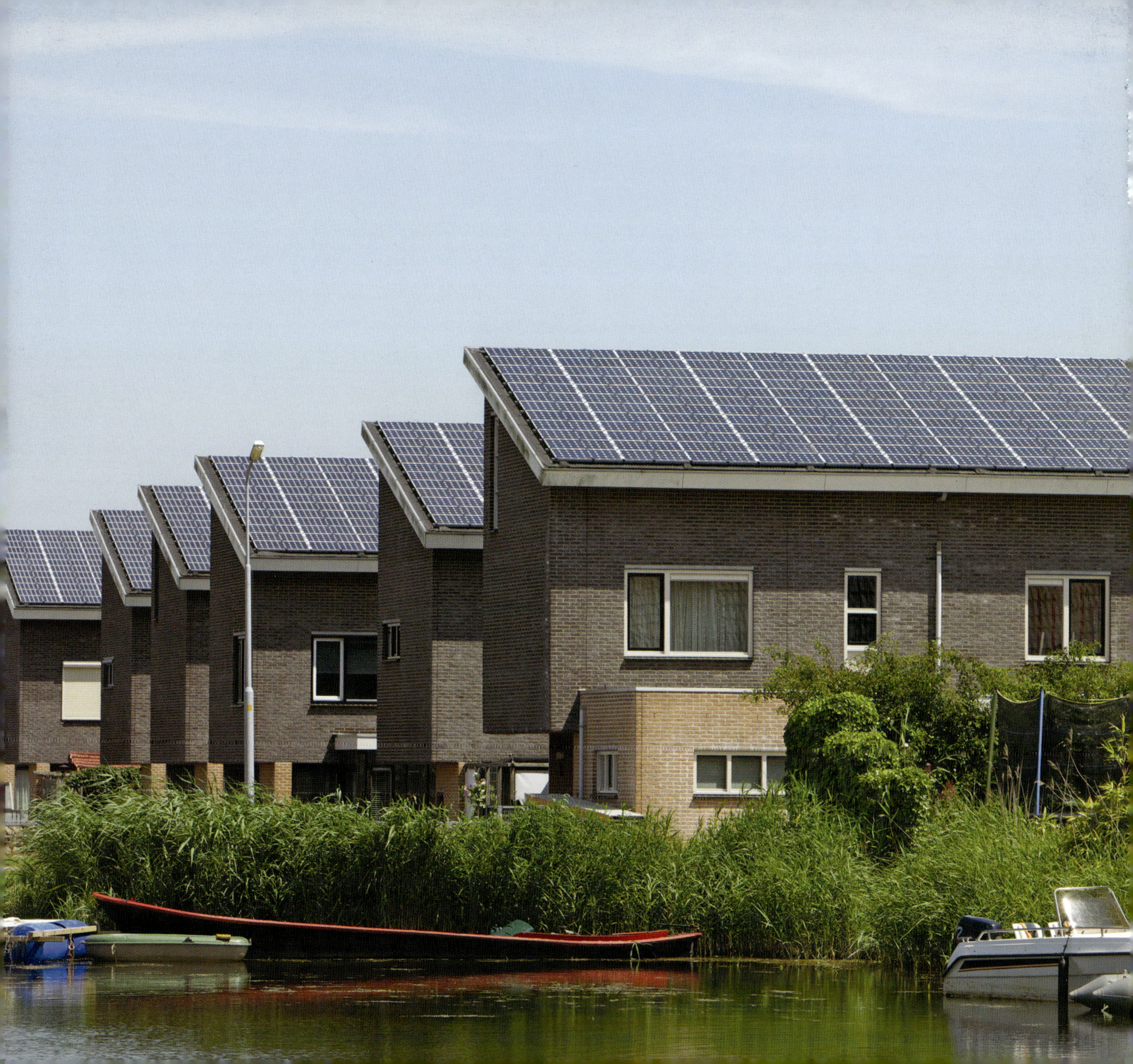

GLOSSARY

BIOFUEL—Fuel made from living or recently living organic matter.

BLACK LIGHT—A device that produces ultraviolet light.

CLIMATE CHANGE—A change in temperature and weather patterns due to human activity such as burning fossil fuels.

FOSSIL FUEL—Fuel formed over millions of years from ancient plant and animal material buried underground, such as coal, oil, and natural gas.

GEOTHERMAL ENERGY—Energy from the heat inside Earth.

GREENHOUSE GAS—A gas, such as carbon dioxide or methane, that contributes to global warming.

HYDROELECTRICITY—Electricity generated by harnessing the energy of moving water.

MICRON—One-millionth of a meter.

NANOMETER—One-billionth of a meter.

NANOPHOTOVOLTAICS—Photovoltaic tools and methods in nanoscale, or a size of 1 to 100 nanometers.

NATURAL GAS—A fossil fuel gas.

NONRENEWABLE RESOURCE—A resource that can't be replenished in a short period of time.

NUCLEAR FUSION—A process that occurs when a substance is so hot that its atoms collide at very high speeds, causing them to gain and lose particles and change from one type of substance to another, releasing massive amounts of energy.

PHOTON—A unit of light energy.

PHOTOVOLTAIC EFFICIENCY—The percentage of energy a solar cell converts into electricity from the sunlight that hits it.

PHOTOVOLTAIC TECHNOLOGY—The tools and methods that convert sunlight directly into electricity.

RENEWABLE RESOURCE—A resource that nature can replace.

SOLAR MODULE—A group of linked solar cells.

THERMAL CAPACITY—The ability to hold heat.

ADDITIONAL RESOURCES

SELECTED BIBLIOGRAPHY

Kryza, Frank T. *The Power of Light: The Epic Story of Man's Quest to Harness the Sun*. New York: McGraw-Hill, 2003. Print.

Smil, Vaclav. *Energy Myths and Realities: Bringing Science to the Energy Policy Debate*. Washington, DC: American Enterprise Institute, 2010. Print.

US Department of Energy. "Energy Explained: Your Guide to Understanding Energy." *U.S. Energy Information Administration*. n.d. Web. 28 Dec. 2011.

US Department of Energy. "History of Solar." *Solar Energy Technologies Program*. n.d. Web. 1 Dec. 2011.

FURTHER READINGS

Marcovitz, Hal. *Can Renewable Energy Replace Fossil Fuels?* San Diego: Reference Point, 2011. Print.

Miller, Debra M. *Energy Production and Alternative Energy*. Farmington Hills, MI: Greenhaven, 2011. Print.

Naff, Clay Farris, ed. *Solar Power*. Farmington Hills, MI: Thomson Gale, 2007. Print.

WEB LINKS

To learn more about solar energy, visit ABDO Publishing Company online at www.abdopublishing.com. Web sites about solar energy are featured on our Book Links page. These links are routinely monitored and updated to provide the most current information available.

FOR MORE INFORMATION

For more information on this subject, contact or visit the following organizations:

ENERGY KIDS
US Department of Energy, Energy Information Administration
1000 Independence Avenue, Washington, DC 20585
202-586-8800
http://www.eia.gov/kids

This organization's Web site is packed with information about energy sources, energy usage, and the history of energy.

NATIONAL RENEWABLE ENERGY LABORATORY EDUCATION PROGRAMS
1617 Cole Boulevard, Golden, CO 80401-3305
303-275-3662
http://www.nrel.gov/education

This organization provides a Web portal to explore sustainable energy solutions.

SOURCE NOTES

CHAPTER 1. SUN POWER

1. "Sun: Read More." *Solar System Exploration*. National Aeronautics and Space Administration, 17 Mar. 2011. Web. 15 Aug. 2012.

2. "Sun: Facts and Figures." *Solar System Exploration*. National Aeronautics and Space Administration, 17 Mar. 2011. Web. 15 Aug. 2012.

3. "Sun: Read More." *Solar System Exploration*. National Aeronautics and Space Administration, 17 Mar. 2011. Web. 15 Aug. 2012.

CHAPTER 2. WHY IS SOLAR POWER IMPORTANT?

1. "Population and Energy Consumption." *World Population Balance*. World Population Balance, n.d. Web. 15 Aug. 2012.

2. "Annual Energy Outlook 2012." *US Energy Information Administration*. US Department of Energy, June 2012. Web. 15 Aug. 2012.

3. Energy in Brief—What Everyone Should Know about Energy: What Is the Role of Coal in the United States? *US Energy Information Administration*. US Department of Energy, 18 July 2012. Web. 15 Aug. 2012.

4. "US Oil Dependence Threatens Security, Economy, Environment." *American Security Project*. American Security Project, 27 May 2010. Web. 15 Aug. 2012.

5. "Is Global Warming Real?" *National Geographic*. National Geographic Society, n.d. Web. 15 Aug. 2012.

6. Brie Loskota. "Solar Cooker Project Evaluation: Iridimi Refugee Camp, Chad." *Solar Cookers International*. Solar Cookers International, Oct. 2007. Web. 7 Jul. 2012.

CHAPTER 3. SOLAR THERMAL ENERGY IN HISTORY

1. Debra Nails. "Socrates." *Stanford Encyclopedia of Philosophy*. Metaphysics Research Lab, CSLI, Stanford University, 9 Nov. 2009. Web. 2 Dec. 2011.

2. Frank T. Kryza. *The Power of Light: The Epic Story of Man's Quest to Harness the Sun*. New York: McGraw-Hill, 2003. Print. 54–58.

3. Ken Butti and John Perlin. "Horace de Saussure and His Hot Boxes of the 1700s." *The Solar Cooking Archive*. Solar Cookers World Network, 1980. Web. 15 Aug. 2012.

4. Ibid.

5. Robert Mabro. "The Oil Weapon: Can It Be Used Today?" *Harvard International Review*. Harvard International Review, 31 Dec. 2007. Web. 6 Jul. 2012.

6. Congressional Quarterly Press Editors. "Chapter 4: Middle Eastern Oil and Gas." *The Middle East, Eleventh Edition*. 2007. Web. 6 Jul. 2012.

CHAPTER 4. PHOTOVOLTAIC TECHNOLOGY IN HISTORY

1. Frank T. Kryza. *The Power of Light: The Epic Story of Man's Quest to Harness the Sun*. New York: McGraw-Hill, 2003. Print. 255.
2. "Tiny Solar Cell Could Make a Big Difference." *National Renewable Energy Library Newsroom*. US Department of Energy, 14 Dec. 2011. Web. 15 Aug. 2012.
3. "Most Efficient Solar Panels." *SRoeCo Solar*. SRoeCo Solar, 19 May 2012. Web. 15 Aug. 2012.
4. Perlin, John. *From Space to Earth: The Story of Solar Electricity*. Cambridge, MA: Harvard University Press, 2002. 54. *Google Book Search*. Web. 15 Aug. 2012.
5. "Federal Support for Solar Energy Consistent with Incentives for Traditional Energy Sources." *SEIA*. Solar Energy Industries Association, 1 May 2012. Web. 15 Aug. 2012.

CHAPTER 5. SMALL BUT MIGHTY: NANOPHOTOVOLTAICS

1. Nanowerk. "Printed Nanotechnology Solar Cells Could Dramatically Reduce Costs." *Nanowerk*. 1 Jul. 2011. Web. 12 Dec. 2011.
2. Joseph Kalowekamo and Erin Baker. "Estimating the Manufacturing Cost of Purely Organic Solar Cells." *Solar Energy* 83.8 (2009). *Erin Baker Faculty Page, University of Massachusetts Amherst*. Web. 15 Aug. 2012.
3. Steve Heckeroth. "The Promise of Thin-Film Solar." *Mother Earth News*. Mother Earth News, Feb.–Mar. 2010. Web. 15 Aug. 2012.
4. Ibid.
5. "Thin-Film Photovoltaic (PV) Cells Market Analysis to 2020—CIGS (Copper Indium Gallium Diselenide) to Emerge as the Major Technology by 2020." *PR Newswire*. PR Newswire Association, 5 Oct. 2011. Web. 15 Aug. 2012.
6. Mike Orcutt. "How Quantum Dots Could Double Solar Cell Efficiency." *Popular Mechanics*. Hearst Communications, 18 Jun. 2010. Web. 15 Aug. 2012.
7. Ibid.
8. Michael Moyer. "The New Dawn of Solar." *Popular Science: Best of What's New '07*. Popular Science, 2007. Web. 15 Aug. 2012.
9. "Mass-Printed Polymer/Fullerene Solar Cells on Paper." *Nanowerk*. Nanowerk, 26 Sep. 2011. Web. 15 Aug. 2012.
10. Michael Graham Richard. "Quote of the Day: Martin Roscheisen, CEO of Nanosolar: Biofuels Don't Cut It." *Treehugger*. Discover Communications, 20 Aug. 2008. Web. 6 Jul. 2012.
11. David L. Chandler. "While You're Up, Print Me a Solar Cell." *MIT News*. Massachusetts Institute of Technology, 11 Jul. 2011. Web. 15 Aug. 2012.
12. Jason Paur. "Solar Airplane to Fly through the Night (Tonight!)." *Wired*. Condé Nast, 7 July 2010. Web. 15 Aug. 2012.

SOURCE NOTES CONTINUED

13. Bruno Giussani. "The Solar-Powered Flight around the Globe." *Wired*. Condé Nast, 16 Mar. 2012. Web. 15 Aug. 2012.

14. Osha Gray Davidson. "Solar-Powered Airplane Makes Historic Flight." *Forbes*. Forbes.com, 13 May 2011. Web. 15 Aug. 2012.

15. James Holloway. "Solar Impulse to Attempt Its Longest, Furthest Flight Yet." *Gizmag*. Gizmag, 29 Mar. 2012. Web. 15 Aug. 2012.

CHAPTER 6. SQUEEZING SUNLIGHT: LUMINESCENT SOLAR CONCENTRATORS

1. "Solar Concentrator Increases Collection with Less Loss." *R&D*. Advantage Business Media, 2 Nov. 2011. Web. 15 Aug. 2012.

CHAPTER 7. HEATING THINGS UP: SOLAR THERMAL INNOVATIONS

1. "CSP World Map—List of CSP Plants." *CSP World*. CSP World, 2012. Web. 15 Aug. 2012.

2. Andy Skumanich. "CSP: Developments in Heat Transfer and Storage Materials." *Renewable Energy Focus*. Elsevier, 13 Apr. 2011. Web. 15 Aug. 2012.

3. Harry Tournemille. "Award-Winning Solar Reflectors Will Cut Production Costs." *Energy Boom*. Energy Boom, 6 Aug. 2009. Web. 15 Aug. 2012.

4. Ibid.

5. Ibid.

6. "Technical." *ReflecTech Mirror Film*. ReflecTech, n.d. Web. 15 Aug. 2012.

7. Rikki Stancich. "Nanofluid Receivers Boost Solar Thermal Efficiency." *CSP Today*. CSP Today, 19 Apr. 2011. Web. 15 Aug. 2012.

8. Rikki Stancich. "Nanofluid Receivers Boost Solar Thermal Efficiency." *CSP Today*. CSP Today, 19 Apr. 2011. Web. 15 Aug. 2012.

9. "Nanoparticles Improve Solar Collection Efficiency." *ScienceDaily*. ScienceDaily, 5 Apr. 2011. Web. 15 Aug. 2012.

10. "Nanoparticles Improve Solar Collection Efficiency." *ScienceDaily*. ScienceDaily, 5 Apr. 2011. Web. 15 Aug. 2012.

11. "Estimating Appliance and Home Electronic Energy Usage." *Energy Savers*. US Department of Energy, 9 Feb. 2011. Web. 15 Aug. 2012.

12. David Biello. "How to Use Solar Energy at Night." *Scientific American*. Scientific American, 18 Feb. 2009. Web. 15 Aug. 2012.

13. Mike McGehee. Message to the author. 25 Jun. 2012. E-mail.

14. David Biello. "How to Use Solar Energy at Night." *Scientific American*. Scientific American, 18 Feb. 2009. Web. 15 Aug. 2012.

15. Julia Layton. "Is There a Way to Get Solar Power at Night?: Andasol 1." *HowStuffWorks.com*. HowStuffWorks, n.d. Web. 15 Aug. 2012.

16. Brett Prior. "Eureka! Italy's Archimede Believes Molten Salt Holds the Key to CSP's Future." *GreenTech Solar*. GreenTech Media, 26 Jan. 2011. Web. 15 Aug. 2012.

17. "Molten Salt Heat Transfer Fluid." *Energy Innovation Portal*. US Department of Energy, 9 Sep. 2011. Web. 15 Aug. 2012.

CHAPTER 8. SOLAR POWER TODAY AND TOMORROW

1. "2010 Renewable Energy Data Book." *National Renewable Energy Laboratory*. US Department of Energy, Sep. 2011. Web. 15 Aug. 2012.

2. "Solar Power Could Provide 10 Percent of U.S. Energy by 2025." *Energy Efficiency and Renewable Energy News*. US Department of Energy, 25 Jun. 2008. Web. 15 Dec. 2012.

3. "2010 Renewable Energy Data Book." *National Renewable Energy Laboratory*. US Department of Energy, Sep. 2011. Web. 15 Aug. 2012.

4. Matthew Knight. "A Dazzling Future for Solar Power?" *CNN*. Cable News Network, 12 May 2010. Web. 15 Aug. 2012.

5. "2010 Renewable Energy Data Book." *National Renewable Energy Laboratory*. US Department of Energy, Sep. 2011. Web. 15 Aug. 2012.

6. Ibid.

7. Ibid.

8. "Solar Power Could Provide 10 Percent of U.S. Energy by 2025." *Energy Efficiency and Renewable Energy News*. US Department of Energy, 25 Jun. 2008. Web. 15 Dec. 2012.

9. Matthew Knight. "A Dazzling Future for Solar Power?" *CNN*. Cable News Network, 12 May 2010. Web. 15 Aug. 2012.

10. Ibid.

INDEX

Adams, William Grylls, 45
Anasazi people, 33, 35
Andasol I, 89, 91, 92
Anthemius of Tralles, 32
Archimede, 93
atmosphere, 10, 22–25, 26, 84
atom, 8, 9, 11

Becquerel, Alexandre-Edmond, 45
Berman, Elliot, 48
Borschberg, André, 68–69

carbon dioxide, 9, 22
Carter, Jimmy, 51
Caux, Salomon de, 35
centralized solar power, 98, 100
Chapin, Daryl, 46
chemical energy, 10, 20
climate change, 23–25
copper indium gallium diselenide, 57, 59, 64

Day, Richard Evans, 45
dish-engine system, 79–80
distributed solar power, 98, 99

electrons, 8, 11, 39, 45, 60, 62

flat-plate solar panels. *See* traditional solar panels
fluorescence, 73, 75
Fritts, Charles, 45–46
Fuller, Calvin, 46

gasoline, 18, 42
global warming. *See* climate change
graphite, 85, 86–88
green energy, 17, 18, 25, 29, 49
greenhouse effect, 23
greenhouse gases, 22–25
grid, 99, 100

heat transfer fluid, 85–89, 91–93
helium, 7–8, 9
Herschel, John, 36
hydrogen, 7–8, 9

Justinian Code, 33

kinetic energy, 8

lenses, 31, 35, 72
Leonardo da Vinci, 35
linear system, 79–80, 82, 92, 93
luminescent solar concentrator (LSC), 71–77

Massachusetts Institute of Technology, 64–66
mirror film, 84
mirrors, 32–33, 35, 38, 72, 80, 82, 84
Mouchot, Augustin, 36, 38

nanophotovoltaics, 54–66
Nanosolar, 63–64
National Renewable Energy Laboratory, 49, 82
neutrons, 8, 9
nuclear fusion, 7, 9

paper solar modules, 64–66
passive solar building design, 12, 32–33, 40
Pearson, Gerald, 46
photosynthesis, 9
Piccard, Bertrand, 68
pollution, 18, 25, 84
potential energy, 8
power tower system, 79–80, 82, 85, 88, 92
protons, 8

quantum dots, 60, 62, 66

Reagan, Ronald, 51
renewable energy, 20, 25, 42, 51
renewable sources, 18, 20

salts, 80, 88–93
Sandia National Laboratories, 93
Saussure, Horace-Bénédict de, 36
SEGS VI, 85
semiconducting nanocrystals, 60
semiconductors, 12, 55, 56, 57, 58, 60, 64, 71
silicon, 11, 26, 46, 54, 57, 58, 64, 68, 77
solar energy challenges, 26–27, 90–91, 99, 100
solar engines, 36, 38–39
Solar Impulse, 68–69
Solar Millennium, 89–90, 93
solar modules, 12, 48–49, 53, 55, 56, 64, 65, 71, 72, 77

solar ponds, 92
solar spectrum, 15
solar thermal energy, 31, 35–36
solar thermal power plants, 12, 43, 79–80, 82, 85, 90–91
solar water heaters, 39–40
steam engines, 36, 38, 42, 87

thin-film solar cells, 54–57, 59
trackers, 72, 77
traditional solar panels, 54, 55–56, 58, 64, 71, 72, 76–77
turbine, 12, 18, 39, 43, 51, 80

Vanguard I, 47

watts, 87
wavelengths, 15, 46, 56, 73, 75, 82, 85

ABOUT THE AUTHOR

Christine Zuchora-Walske has been writing and editing books and magazines for children and their parents for 20 years. Her author credits include natural science titles; books exploring the world's nations; a debate on Internet censorship; books on pregnancy and parenting; and more. Christine has also edited hundreds of articles and books in many genres and for all ages. Christine is especially fond of science and history. But she loves all kinds of knowledge and literature. She never tires of learning new things, and she gets a kick out of trading knowledge with others.

ABOUT THE CONTENT CONSULTANT

Michael McGehee is an associate professor of Materials Science and Engineering at Stanford University. He is director of the Center for Advanced Molecular Photovoltaics. He received his PhD in materials science from the University of California-Santa Barbara.